"ARE YOU THERE?" SHE WHISPERED INTO THE BLACKNESS OF THE DARKENED CONSERVATORY.

"Darling," the marquess murmured in a low voice, turning her around to face him.

Sally could feel her bones beginning to melt as she felt her body pressed closely against him. Her mantle, which she had been carrying over one arm, fell unheeded to the floor.

And then his lips came down on hers, burning this time, and exploring, causing dizzying skyrockets to burst in her brain. His mouth left hers and began to wander over her face, kissing her closed eyelids, the tip of her nose, her ears, and her neck.

In a tiny corner of Sally's brain alarm bells were beginning to ring. Thoughts jumbled one over the other. She was alone with him without a chaperon. He was kissing her only because she had appeared easy game. His hand left her waist and slid down the low front of her dress, cupping her bosom in a warm clasp.

"No!" cried Sally, wrenching herself free. "You mustn't . . . you frighten me!"

SALLY

*Marion Chesney writing as
Jennie Tremaine*

A DELL BOOK

Published by
Dell Publishing Co., Inc.
1 Dag Hammarskjold Plaza
New York, New York 10017

Dell ® TM 681510, Dell Publishing Co., Inc.

ISBN: 0-440-17523-2

Printed in the United States of America

One Previous Edition

March 1988

10 9 8 7 6 5 4 3 2 1

KRI

FOR RACHEL FEVOLA,
WITH LOVE

CHAPTER ONE

It all began the morning the baby was sick on the breakfast table—a small thing to start such a revolution in the mind of Sally Blane, but it was just the last of many things that made her decide she was better off living on her own.

Sally had come to live with her married sister, Emily, a year ago, and already it seemed like a lifetime. She had been with her parents in India when they had died. Emily, already married some ten years, had remained behind with her husband George Bessamy, a solicitor, in Sussex. Emily was a mature thirty and mother of five, and Sally was unwed, being a mere eighteen years of age.

The girls' parents, Colonel and Mrs. Anthony Blane, had died at a dinner party in Bombay at which the host's British-hating Indian cook had put arsenic in the mulligatawny.

Fortunately for Sally, she was not present at the dinner. Her father had never believed in saving a penny, and after his mess bills were paid, there was enough left to pay for orphan Sally's passage home, leaving only two hundred pounds sterling to set her up in life.

Sally had hoped that some handsome young man would be traveling on the same P & O ship and would promptly propose marriage. But although there were plenty of young officers going home on leave, none seemed to want even to flirt with the small girl with her hair scraped back into two braids.

Emily had welcomed Sally into her home in Churchwold, in Sussex, appointed her unpaid nursery maid, and seemed to expect her to be content with that lot until the children should grow up. Sally was small and slight with a wistful little face and huge gray eyes. She had masses of light-brown hair, which, so far, no one had ever suggested she wear up. It flowed down her back in a rather Burne-Jones manner, and on Sundays it was sedately confined at the nape of her neck with a large satin bow.

Emily was the model of the Edwardian matron, heavy in the bust, placid in the face, and empty in the upperworks. She was a ferociously dedicated mother. Her whole life was devoted to turning out model children, and as a result they were all quite horribly miserable and spoiled. Peter, the eldest of the brood, was ten; Paul, eight; Mary, seven; Joseph, five; and then there was baby Marmaduke, aged two. The children had no hope of any discipline from their father, since George Bessamy left early in the morning for his offices in Lewes, not returning until seven in the evening, by which time the little monsters were all in bed. On Sundays, after he had been to church, George retired to his study and locked the door, not emerging until the evening, rather slurred of speech and baggy of eye.

Sally tried hard to like the children and pay for her keep by attending to their wants, but as she was not allowed to raise her voice to them or smack them or reproach them in any way, they tormented her mercilessly.

Had she had any friends or social life, her lot might have been easier, but Churchwold was a small village with a population of retired gentlepeople living mostly on small pensions. Their entertainments consisted of gossiping maliciously over pots of weak tea and dry salmon sandwiches. There were several other young spinsters of the parish, but to Sally's amazement they seemed, unlike herself, to have become reconciled to their lot and rattled their cups and gossiped as heartily as their elders.

It was a very damp village, one of those English villages that look so beautiful on calendars but are so unpleasant to live in. The pretty Tudor houses with their thatch and beams and wattle smelled of dry rot, and the sanitation had not changed much since the time of The Virgin Queen. The vicar was constantly trying to raise funds to restore the roof of the church, but no one showed any interest, not even when one of the carved angels on the hammer beam ceiling fell down one day and brained poor Mrs. Anstruther, striking her dead.

Mrs. Anstruther had been ninety and had lived long enough, the congregation had pointed out, turning neglect into some sort of divine euthanasia.

There were two greengrocers in the village, one at one end, mostly patronized by the inbred poor, and one at the other end for the gentry.

Both sold exactly the same goods at the same prices, and no one could say for sure why the one got the posh trade and the other the peasant. The posh grocers also housed the village post office, which was open at mysterious hours and always seemed to be closed when one wanted to mail a particularly heavy parcel. There was a public house, which exuded a strong aroma of stale meat pies and strong beer.

Sally had tried hard to accustom herself to her lot. But now the full horror of the summer holidays was brought home to her. The children would be in and around her all day. Not only that, but the Bessamys would be making their annual pilgrimage to Brighton for two weeks, and to Sally that meant two weeks of running up and down the beach after her charges and trying not to hope that a tidal wave might drown them all.

It was not the children's tempers that frayed Sally's nerves but their constant whining. They were great whiners right down to Baby Marmaduke, who had a particularly grating call.

It began to dawn on Sally that apart from housemaids and parlormaids and such like, there was a new breed of women who were beginning to take jobs and earn their own livings.

On the day she made up her mind—or rather the day Baby Marmaduke made it up for her—Sally was seated at the breakfast table on a particularly blazing-hot August morning, trying to read the *Daily Bugle* to shut out the chorus of complaint that was going on around her.

Emily sat drinking tea contentedly, deaf to the whining of her children, as only a rather stupid and devoted mother could be.

Peter was picking at his spots, Paul was exploring the inside of his rather large nose with one finger, Mary was crying dismally because she could not have a new lace dress, and Joseph had caught a bluebottle and was drowning it in the honey pot. Only Marmaduke had not given tongue, since he had thrown his kippers to the cat and was watching that animal chewing them up under his high chair with wide-eyed interest.

Suddenly all sound vanished for Sally as she stared at the paper. On the front page was a political report from the Lobby Correspondent, Mrs. Mary Service. Sally's eyes widened. A woman—a Lobby Correspondent! A woman stalking through that masculine preserve of the House of Commons, taking notes!

I could work, she thought suddenly. *I could earn my own money. I could be free.* Sally thought feverishly. She knew she could write, for in Bombay, hadn't she been chosen out of all the girls to edit the school magazine?

She could see it now: *the Annual Magazine of the Misses Lelongs' Seminary for the Daughters of Officers and Gentlemen*—Editor, Miss Sally Blane.

And then Baby Marmaduke was sick. Right over the newspaper. Right down the front page.

Sally put down the wreck of the newspaper and stared at Emily, who was looking out the window into the garden with large, calflike eyes.

"Emily," she said, "have I any money?"

"What, dear?" said her sister vaguely above the whines of her offspring. "Money? Well, two hundred pounds, darling. That was all that was left. George banked it for you."

"That will do," said Sally, getting to her feet. "Oh, shut up!" she yelled at the assorted brood. "I, Emily, am going to London, and I am going to get a job—with a newspaper."

15

"Oh, really, darling!" said Emily. "How nice. Oh, Marmaduke, what a mess you have made."

"I want my two hundred today!" yelled Sally, turning pink with excitement.

"Well, dear . . . oh, *Mary*, Mummy shall get you the dress if it means so much . . . you will find the bankbook in George's desk . . . Peter! Stop pinching Paul . . ."

Sally almost ran from the room to George's study. After some scrabbling she found a bankbook made out in her name from the Sussex and South Down Bank, Lewes. Sally felt feverish. She could not wait. Not one more day. She had to leave. Escape. *Now.*

She ran to her room and began to pack a suitcase, cramming as many things into it as she could. It was still only nine o'clock in the morning. Plenty of time to start a new life before dark. She crammed a sailor hat on her head and, seizing her suitcase, ran down the stairs, straight out the front door, and down the crunchy gravel of the drive as fast as she could, in case Emily should stop her.

Past the name board of the house, *Mon Repos;* past the dusty laurel hedge; down the hot, dusty road to the village; past the blind eyes of the

Victorian villas, like Emily's; past the squat crouch of the thatched cottages; and past the poor grocers and along the village street to the rich grocers to try to catch someone, *anyone*, to give her a lift into Lewes. There was Squire Roberts in his dogcart. Splendid! The fat and florid squire looked somewhat surprised at her peremptory demand to be taken to Lewes but nonetheless told Sally to hop up.

Caution came to Sally's fevered brain just in time. In answer to the squire's questions, she told him she was taking a suitcase of old clothes into her brother-in-law George's office, since he wanted the clothes for some charity or other.

Heat shimmered over the fields, burning away the cool breath of morning. The sky arched above, hot and cloudless, and dust rose in little eddies from the road. Soon the squat majesty of Lewes Castle loomed ahead, and Sally fretted while the squire negotiated the cobble-stoned streets, insisting on setting her down at the door of George's office.

She hid in the doorway until the squire had clattered off, and then went out in search of the bank.

Blow! Dash it!—and all other horrible epithets. The bank manager would not release the money without a signed letter from George!

Sally went back out into the street and stood scowling horribly. George was not vague like Emily. George would be pompous and stupid and obstructive simply because he was pompous, stupid, and obstructive about everything.

She made her way back to George's office and mounted the dusty steps. There were two clerks in the outer office, who stood up as she entered the room, dragging her suitcase behind her.

Mr. Bessamy, they said, was with a client. But if Miss Blane would take a seat for a few moments? Miss Blane would.

Sally sat down at a small desk in the corner and poked about idly. Then she saw a sheaf of headed business paper, a pen, and ink.

Taking out a piece of stationery, Sally dipped the steel pen in the inkwell and began to write.

Some ten minutes later George ushered out his client and then frowned in surprise to see Sally waiting for him.

"What are you doing here, Miss Blane?" He never called her Sally.

"Emily wants you to sign this letter. It's a list of things for some charity."

George fumbled in his top pocket for his pince-nez. "Don't worry about *reading* it," said Sally anxiously. "Just *sign*."

"I never sign anything that I have not read," said George stiffly. Sally saw her hopes of a career crashing about her ears.

"Give it to me," said George, holding out a well-manicured hand.

"I do not know what Emily is thinking about," he went on crossly as he took the letter and adjusted his pince-nez. "A young girl like yourself should not be here alone. Gladys should have been sent with you." Gladys was the parlormaid.

Please, prayed Sally wildly. *Please . . . please . . . oh, please . . .*

The door opened and a majestic woman sailed in, followed by her maid.

"I," she announced, "am Lady Farringer. Mr. Bessamy, I presume?"

George moved forward, his thin body bent in an obsequious curve.

"Yes, I have that honor, Lady Farringer."

"Good! Good!" exclaimed that lady, wheezing like a pug. "You have been highly recommended to me by the Cartwrights. Let's not waste time! To business! To business!"

"Indeed, my lady, right away," said George.

"My letter," said Sally.

George glared at her. "Oh, very well," he said, dipping a pen quickly into the inkwell on one of his clerk's desks and scrawling his signature on the bottom. "Wait for me here, Miss Blane, and we will go over this together later. Ah, Lady Farringer! Step this way!"

They vanished into his office, and Sally seized the precious letter, which, of course, was one authorizing her to draw two hundred pounds, and fled.

Ten-thirty already! And what an age they took at the bank. She stuffed the notes haphazardly into her reticule, causing the teller to shake his head mournfully, and then ran all the way to the railway station, her suitcase bumping against her legs.

She was just in time for the 11:15 train to London, Victoria.

She sank wearily into a third-class compartment just as the train began to chug its way out of the station. It was only then that she realized the compartment was shared by a tired, jaded mother and her three children who were returning home after their annual holiday. The compartment seemed to be bulging with buckets and spades, seaweed and shells, parasols, and jammy, sticky fingers.

"I don't like you," said the imp opposite Sally with an ingratiating leer.

"Now, Freddie," said its mother with an indulgent smile, "don't be so forward."

Sally simply closed her eyes and pretended to go to sleep. The children, after trying shouting in her ear pulling her hair, and kicking her shins eventually gave up and left her in peace so that at last, overcome by the stuffy heat, she actually did fall asleep, not awakening until the train was running in over the houses of London. Over the river it roared with a long, wailing whistle and plunged headlong into the sooty depths of Victoria Station, like a great iron animal returning to its burrow.

Sally felt quite shaky and groggy. The noise and bustle of the great station made her feel very small. Surely it would be better to go back, back to Emily, back to Sussex. Already distance was lending her sister's home enchantment. But her companions of the journey surged past her,

21

whining and moaning and kicking and reminding her vividly of what she had left behind, so Sally stiffened her small spine, picked up her suitcase, and marched to the cab rank.

"The *Daily Bugle*," she said, climbing into one and settling herself with a sigh of relief in the musty interior of the hansom.

Fleet Street was, and is, the home of British newspapers. A narrow, crowded street crammed with newspaper and magazine offices, it runs from the Law Courts at the Temple down to Ludgate Circus. Of course, some newspapers may have their headquarters outside this magic canyon, but for a budding newspaperwoman there is nothing like the Street itself.

On this hot day as Sally paid off the hansom and picked up her suitcase, it seemed to be full of people bustling to and fro importantly.

There was an exotic smell of hot paper, and the pavement beneath her feet trembled slightly to the thud of the great printing presses. Sally looked up at the great gilt clock over the ornate offices of the *Daily Bugle*. One o'clock. Her stomach rumbled, reminding her it was lunchtime. The editor would surely be out for lunch.

Drat! And Sally wanted only the editor. No one else would do.

She took herself off across the road to a cafeteria and sat for two miserable hours in its hot, flyblown interior over two cups of tea and a currant bun. George once said that business executives always took two hours for lunch.

At precisely three o'clock Sally pushed her damp hair out of her eyes, pressed her now crumpled sailor hat firmly on her head, and made her way through the press of horse traffic to the offices of the *Daily Bugle*.

But the uniformed man in the front hall quickly disabused her of any idea of marching up the marble stairs and into the lift and on to the editor's office. "You 'as to 'ave an appointment, miss," he said, sneering, and then returned to his crossword, obviously dismissing her from his mind.

Sally gazed at the oiled top of his bent head in a baffled way. And then she said quietly, "He will be disappointed if he does not see me . . . Uncle will, I mean."

"Uncle!" The man's head jerked up. "You mean ter say as how Mr. Wingles is yer uncle?"

"Yes," said Sally firmly. "I have just arrived

from India. When he last wrote to me, he told me to come straight to the office."

"Oh, well, harrumph. In that case, miss, you'd better go right up. 'Ere, Joey!" he said to a small, pert office boy. "This 'ere is Mr. Wingles's niece. Take 'er up."

Still clutching her suitcase, her heart beating swiftly, Sally followed Joey into the small lift. Joey slammed the gates shut with a clang. She had crossed the Rubicon. No going back now.

In the editor's outer office a grim female was typing furiously. She unbent on hearing that Sally was the editor's niece and said she would inform Mr. Wingles of Sally's arrival. She did not ask Sally's name. The fact that the girl was the editor's niece was enough.

In no time at all Sally found herself in the man's presence.

Mr. Wingles was a tall, muscular Scot with ferocious eyebrows.

He took one look at the trembling Sally, with her crumpled sailor hat, her battered suitcase, and her girlish hair flowing down the back of her tailored suit.

"Another of 'em," he snorted with disgust. "No jobs for you, lassie. Get back to your ma."

He rang the bell, and the grim secretary leapt in with the alacrity of a jack-in-the-box. "Miss Fleming," said the editor awfully. "Take this wee lassie away and send her packing. It's a new trick. This is not my niece."

"Wait!" cried Sally desperately. "I can write. I have had work published!"

"Indeed! And where may I ask have you had your writing published?"

Sally took a deep breath. "In the *Annual Magazine of the Misses Lelong Seminary for the Daughters of Officers and Gentlemen* . . . in Bombay. I was the editor."

Mr. Wingles leaned back in his chair. "In the —" He began to laugh and laugh. "In the—in the—"

Miss Fleming ushered Sally out grimly, leaving the editor gasping for words.

"Now, look here, young woman," said Miss Fleming. "Tricks like the one you just played could cost me my job. How dare you!"

Sally's courage fled. She felt young and silly and alone and frightened. Large unchecked tears began to roll down her cheeks.

"Oh, goodness!" said Miss Fleming impatiently. "Here, have a handkerchief and sit down." She waited while Sally gulped and sobbed herself into silence.

"Now," said Miss Fleming, adjusting her cardboard wrist protectors, "you'd better tell me about it. You are too young to be running about London on your own."

And so Sally told her all about it. About Emily and the children and about seeing the name of the Lobby Correspondent on the front page.

"Mrs. Service, our Lobby Correspondent," said Miss Fleming in a dry voice, "is by way of being a relative of the newspaper owner, Lord Picken—if you take my meaning. Now be a good girl and go back home. For all you may think, it's a man's world. Where would a young thing like you stay on her own? Do you have relatives in London?"

Sally shook her head miserably.

"Then just go home, there's a good child," said Miss Fleming in a softer voice.

Sally nodded dumbly and picked up her suitcase. She turned toward the door wearily. But the little imp who looks after budding journalists was not going to let her escape so easily. And somewhere at the bottom of Sally's misery he planted a small seed of hope.

Standing with her head drooping and her hand on the handle, Sally said in a low voice, "Well, one day I'll make it. Miss Fleming, do you have relatives in London? If you will excuse the personal question."

Miss Fleming sighed and took off her horn-rimmed glasses and patted her iron-gray hair. "No, child. I am one of the many businesswomen who fend for themselves. I live in a lodging house in Twenty-two Bryant's Court, off Leicester Square. One small room and a gas ring. I would gladly throw it up for a home and a garden—even if that home was full of someone else's children.

"Good-bye," said Sally meekly. "I will take your kind advice."

Miss Fleming looked at the small, elflike, tear-stained face, at the heavy battered suitcase, at the dusty boots. "Come back and see me when you're in London again," she said with a sudden smile, which lit up her harsh features. "I'll treat you to an ice at Gunter's."

"Thank you," said Sally, smiling back. "I won't forget."

Miss Fleming shook her head and went back to her typing. Sally trailed down by way of the stairs, not having the courage to operate the lift herself.

She stood on the burning pavement outside, irresolute. Newsboys were already crying the evening papers' headlines.

That little spark of hope was growing into a flame. No, Sally would not give up so easily. She went up to a newsagent's kiosk and bought a map of London and, standing on the hot pavement, looked up Bryant's Court. She turned to look for a hansom, for although Leicester Square and its environs was within walking distance, her case felt heavier by the minute.

But as she turned around toward the street the sunlight was shining on a small brass plaque at the side of a doorway in one of the courts that led off Fleet Street. Sally was immature enough to be superstitious, and she immediately felt that that plaque had been lit up expressly for some reason.

She looked up at the name of the court— Haggen's Court—and then walked forward, shadowing the plaque with her body so that she could read the name.

HOME CHATS read the curly legend. THE FAMILY MAGAZINE.

She took a deep breath and pushed open the door. A steep flight of wooden steps led upward, and Sally toiled up it, bumping her suitcase against the walls. At the top she almost collided with an ink-stained young man. He took one look at her tear-stained face and schoolgirlish dress.

"Agony," he said obscurely. "Mrs. Hepplewhite. Through there. Don't tell her I sent you."

There was a frosted glass door with a legend in black lettering: AUNT MABEL. LETTERS EDITOR.

Sally shrugged wearily. It was a beginning. She pushed open the door.

A little elderly gray-haired lady started in alarm and quickly thrust a bottle and a glass into the top drawer of her desk.

"Yeees?" she said in a soft, genteel voice.

"My name is Miss Blane," said Sally, "and I want a job."

"Did you write to me?" asked Mrs. Hepplewhite, alias Aunt Mabel, peering myopically at Sally.

"No," said Sally flatly.

There was a long silence. Aunt Mabel sighed. "I have no time to speak to you," she said at last. "I have so many, many letters to deal with. So many sinners. Take this one." She held out a piece of cheap notepaper covered with tear-blotched, illiterate scrawl. "This is from some housemaid who has become . . . er . . . tut-tut . . . pregnant. She wants my advice.

"I shall tell her she must read two chapters of her Bible every day for the rest of her life and to report immediately to the Society for Fallen Mothers."

Sally thought privately that this was the most heartless piece of advice she had ever heard but nonetheless sat down, first because she had given up hope and saw Emily and the children looming closer, and second because she was tired.

"Yes, yes," dithered Aunt Mabel, looking slyly at Sally and producing both the glass and the bottle out of the top drawer again. "Medicine," she explained, although Sally thought Aunt Mabel's medicine smelled remarkably like gin.

"Now, here's another . . . yes . . . yes . . ." went on Aunt Mabel after fortifying herself from the bottle without resorting to the glass. "Young lady is being forced to marry rich neighbor's son. Does not want to. Ungrateful girl! Shall tell her marriages are not made in Heaven but by sensible parents. Honor thy father and thy mother—hic!"

Aunt Mabel began to search feverishly among the letters on her desk. "My spectacles. Now, where did I put them?" she demanded.

Sally looked around helpfully. The room was cluttered with filing cabinets piled high with yellowing copies of *Home Chats*.

Sally remembered the magazine now, for Emily's cook took it for the recipes. It had a strong religious flavor and a very small circulation.

There was a small gas fire and oak bookshelves on one wall, and various religious pictures decorated the other three, which were of the highly colored variety, in which a blond-and-blue-eyed Jesus divided loaves and fishes, walked on the water, and suffered the little children to come unto Him.

Then Sally saw the spectacles on the dusty mantelshelf. "There they are," she said, rising to her feet. "I'll get them for you."

"No! No!" cried Aunt Mabel, springing to her

feet with surprising agility. "I never let anyone touch my spectacles." She took one tottering step toward the fireplace and then clutched her heart. She cast a look of watery eyed surprise on Sally, and then fell headlong, her head striking the black iron fender around the gas fire with a sickening crack.

"Help!" called Sally desperately. "*Help!*"

The frosted glass door was pushed open and a bluff, middle-aged man smelling strongly of beer came striding into the room.

He brushed past Sally and bent over the fallen body of Aunt Mabel.

"Dead as a doornail," he grunted, "and she didn't even write her column, and it's got to go to press tonight. Well, got to get the doctor."

Sally sat in a daze as first a policeman arrived to take her statement, then a doctor, then a clutch of weeping relatives. Finally the body was removed, and the bluff man who introduced himself as the Editor, Mr. Barton, and Sally were left alone.

"Poor old thing," he said, shaking his head. "The gin did her in. Now, what am I to do? There'll be no Aunt Mabel column this time."

"I'll do it," said Sally, feeling dizzy and

32

strange after the shock of seeing the sudden death of Aunt Mabel.

"You! You're a schoolgirl," said Mr. Barton.

"I'm eighteen," said Sally briskly, going round and sitting behind the desk and picking up the first letter. "And you haven't got anyone else."

"That's true," he said wearily. "Oh, very well. Short answers. Tell 'em to read their Bible. Be back at seven o'clock for it, and if you can't do it . . . well, we wouldn't have an Aunt Mabel column anyway until I found someone else."

Sally worked on in a frenzy after he had gone. She answered all the letters in the manner in which she would like an answer to her own problems, delving into her vast knowledge culled in the Bombay kitchens of marriage and death and childbirth.

She wrote rapidly in neat script, and when Mr. Barton returned at seven, she proudly handed him the completed manuscript.

Fortunately for Sally, he read her first reply, which was fairly orthodox, and grunted his approval. "Pretty touch," he said gruffly. "Pity you can't have the job. Too young."

"I'll call tomorrow for my money," said Sally.

"What money?"

"The money you owe me for being Aunt Mabel," said Sally patiently.

"Oh . . . that. Oh, all right. G'night."

Sally picked up her suitcase wearily and walked down the stairs, out into the court, and out into Fleet Street.

She flagged a passing four-wheeler.

"Bryant's Court," she said.

Miss Fleming leaned out of her window at the end of the cul-de-sac that was Bryant's Court, trying to find a breath of air.

She heard a harsh altercation directly below and looked down. A small figure in a crumpled sailor hat was arguing with the landlady, Mrs. Goody.

"It's all right, Mrs. Goody," called Miss Fleming. "I'll vouch for her. She's a working girl."

"Oh, very well, mum," sniffed Mrs. Goody. "If you say it's all right, but you 'as to be careful, some o' 'em not bein' what they should be an' . . ."

Her voice trailed away as she led Sally into the lodging. Miss Fleming met Sally on the stairs and held out her hand.

"Well, well," she said. "Welcome to the club."

Sally grinned and then burst into tears.

It was such fun being a working woman!

CHAPTER TWO

Mr. George Bessamy shook out his napkin, picked up his knife and fork, and then put them down again.

The children had been taken off to their rooms by one of the two housemaids. One of them was wailing out into the still evening air—but then, one of them always did.

"My dear," he said to his wife, who was pushing food into her mouth with single-minded absorption, "I was so carried away with the news of my illustrious client that I quite forgot to tell you about Miss Blane."

"Sally?" mumbled Emily vaguely. "What about Sally?"

"Your sister walked into my office this morning, carrying a suitcase and asking me to sign a letter to some charity."

"Did she, dear?"

"What charity?"

"I couldn't really say," said Emily placidly. "She was not concerned about charities this morning. She said something about wanting that two hundred pounds so that she could go to London and become a newspaperwoman. Quite touching, really. At her age, I wanted to become a nun."

Mr. Bessamy glared at his uncaring wife and rose abruptly from the table and headed for the study. In a few moments he was back.

"Mrs. Bessamy," he said awfully. "Miss Blane's bankbook is gone. I think she tricked me into signing a letter to the bank manager. *I* think the thankless girl has gone to London!"

"Don't be silly," said the wife of his bosom with unimpaired calm. "Sally would never behave like that."

Gladys came into the room, looking flushed and agitated. "There's a telegraph boy at the door, mum. Says he has a wire for you."

"Very well, Gladys. Mr. Bessamy, give

Gladys sixpence for the boy, and, Gladys, bring the wire to me."

The maid went out, and Emily began to hum tunelessly between her teeth while her husband rapped his fingers nervously on the table.

When Gladys came back with the wire Mr. Bessamy held out his hand for it. It was inconceivable that a mere woman should be allowed to read something as important as a wire, even if it were addressed to her.

"Heavens!" he exclaimed. "This is monstrous!"

Emily signaled placidly to Gladys to remove the plates and bring in the pudding, blind to the fact that her husband had not even started his dinner.

Mr. Bessamy glared at his wife. "This is from your sister. She says she has found lodgings and a job. Monstrous!"

"Oh, how clever of her!" said Emily.

"She also says she drew out the whole of the two hundred pounds!"

"Well, it is her money."

"Nonsense! That was for Peter's school fees."

"But, my dear, how could you use Sally's money?"

"I should have asked her for it," said Mr. Bessamy, breathing heavily. "Miss Blane *owed* us two hundred pounds for her keep alone!"

"I suppose so," said Emily. "What shall we do?"

"Never, ever speak to her again!"

"It certainly will be rather hard to speak to her, since she is in London and we are in Sussex," said Emily, all mad reason. "She was not much help with the children. In fact, I sometimes think dear Sally did not *like* them, although I know that must be very hard to believe. I shall send on the rest of her clothes and things. I wonder if she wants her teddy, or should I let Marmaduke have it? She is really rather old for a toy, you know, but she was quite sentimental about it . . . my dear?"

But Emily spoke to the open air. For Mr. Bessamy, with a great grinding of teeth, had removed himself to the solace of his study.

Sally smiled weakly at Miss Fleming, who had supplied her with a supper of tinned salmon sandwiches and strong tea after she had sent a wire to Emily. "So you see," ended Sally, who had been regaling her new friend with the story of Aunt Mabel's death, "I don't think I have the job. And how much money should I ask?"

"If I were you," said Miss Fleming firmly, "I would go to bed and have a good night's sleep, and then, in the morning, I would simply turn up at *Home Chats* and start answering the letters. I would tell this Mr. Barton that in the heat of the moment he gave you the job. These Fleet Street men can never remember a thing from one moment to the next."

"I'll try," said Sally doubtfully. "Can I have a bath?"

"If no one's in the bathroom, yes," said Miss Fleming. "You will need two pennies for the geyser, and you'll find the bathroom at the end of the corridor. Now I'll take you back to your room. You're very lucky to get it, you know. It's pretty awful, but it's cheap and clean."

She said good night outside Sally's door, and Sally went into the dark little cell that was to be her home. Tomorrow she would take in her surroundings but just for the moment she was too tired. She undressed, and putting on her dressing gown and slippers, she picked up her sponge bag and made her way along the corridor to the bathroom.

The geyser, fed by two pennies put into the slot, went off with a terrifying bang. The gas roared horrendously, and then a thin stream of boiling water began to trickle out of the brass spout.

Sally sighed. It would take at least half an hour's time to fill.

The bathroom was a long coffin of a place with a high ceiling on which flakes of paint and cobwebs moved in the hot air rising from the gas jets. The cork bath mat was crumbling at the edge, and there was no toilet. That was housed at the opposite end of the corridor. The bathroom was also full of signs: PLEASE LEAVE THE BATH AS YOU WOULD WISH TO FIND IT. EXTINGUISH GAS. USE YOUR OWN SOAP.

Sally waited patiently while the water mounted slowly in the large old tub. The house was full of noises and voices. A woman clattered down the stairs, laughing shrilly and talking nonstop to a silent partner. Somewhere a couple was arguing fiercely, the words mercifully indistinct. There was the sad, pathetic wail of a young baby. There was a mixture of odors of gas, disinfectant, dry rot, mildew, baked potatoes, welks, baked beans, and sour milk. Each room carried

41

the stern warning NO COOKING IN THE ROOMS, but according to Miss Fleming, no one paid any attention. They all used a little gas ring that pulled out next to the gas fire and on it cooked their suppers.

At last the bath was ready, and by that time there were several impatient rattles at the door and cries of "Hurry up in there! Are you going to take all night?"

"I've only just run the bath!" called Sally, but this only produced more furious rattlings at the door, so instead of having a long, leisurely soak, she had a hurried scrub, and, after cleaning out the bath, she opened the door to be confronted with six pairs of furious eyes, three male sets and three female. Sally blushed at being seen attired only in her nightgown and woolly dressing gown by the opposite sex, but the men were too impatient and would not have noticed if she had emerged stark naked.

Once in the darkness of her room—NO GAS TO BE LIT AFTER 10 P.M.—Sally turned back the thin covers of the iron bed and then went to lean out of the window.

Below her in Bryant's Court the ladies of the night were plying their trade. Sally raised her eyes instead and looked over the rooftops, where London lay spread out under an orange sky.

The very air seemed to pulsate with raucous life. She sent up a prayer for the soul of Aunt Mabel, and then gave herself up to dreams of the future. She was in London and everything was possible. Good-bye, Emily.

She would never go back.

Mr. Barton, Editor of *Home Chats,* paused at the top of the stairs. He saw a shadow moving behind the frosted glass of the Letter Editor's door and went forward and pushed it open.

Sally, with her hair carefully piled on top of her small head, was going over the filing cabinets with a feather duster.

"What are you doing here?" demanded Mr. Barton crossly.

"Don't you remember?" said Sally sweetly, although her heart was hammering against her ribs. "You gave me Aunt Mabel's job."

"I did?" Mr. Barton clutched his head. It had been a hectic evening, what with the old girl dying like that, and then putting the magazine to bed. He'd had a few more pints than were good for him, and so the evening before came back to him as a sort of gray fuzziness interspersed with bright flashes of total recall.

He could remember the head printer laughing over the Aunt Mabel column and pronouncing it very good.

He looked at Sally doubtfully. Had he offered her the job?

She certainly looked less of a schoolgirl with her hair up. In fact, she looked very attractive indeed. Enough to make the Reverend Frobisher Entwhistle turn in his grave. The Reverend Entwhistle had founded the magazine some fifty years ago. The small profit from the journal went into a trust for his various dissolute offspring. Mr. Barton had held the job for the past twenty years. He had tried to storm Fleet Street as a young man with dreams of becoming a foreign correspondent burning in his eyes. But somehow he had become the editor of *Home Chats* instead. He had made no changes.

Apart from Aunt Mabel, an office boy, and Mr. Barton, the rest of the contributors were free-lance, sending in articles on "How to Reprimand a Bad Servant," "How to Raise Funds for Your Local Church," "Parish Gossip," and similar epistles.

He himself wrote the cookery column, plagiarizing Mrs. Beeton without the smallest shred of conscience. He lived for the evenings, which he spent at the bar of the Red Lion around the corner, when, after the fifth pint, he could pretend he was a real Fleet Street man and hint darkly at scoops in far countries with all the other failures who were doing exactly the same thing.

Suddenly the whole morning-after futility of his job hit him.

"Very well," he said to Sally. "But only a trial, mind. We only publish six letters and answers. But you have to reply personally to everything that comes in."

"Is there a lot of correspóndence?" asked Sally anxiously, looking around the cluttered room.

"No," sighed Mr. Barton. "Aunt Mabel was too much of a Bible-basher to be popular. If you run short, make 'em up."

"Isn't that dishonest?" asked Sally, round-eyed.

Mr. Barton stared at her in disgust. "If you want to work in Fleet Street," he said caustically, "you'd better learn the ropes. I am not asking you to report on wars that don't exist or social scandals that never happened, although there's plenty of those in the popular press. If you don't have letters, write them yourself. That's not selling your soul."

Sally nodded. He stared at her, and then he said, "And another thing—*don't,* whatever you do, tell anyone you're Aunt Mabel. You're too young, see! We've got a drawing of this sweet little old lady with specs at the top of the column, and that's what you're supposed to look like."

"What are my wages?" asked Sally faintly.

"Two pounds and fifteen shillings a week," he said. "Take it or leave it."

"I'll take it," said Sally breathlessly. It seemed like an awful lot of money to her, and she had hardly made a dent in her fortune of two hundred pounds.

Mr. Barton gave a weary flip of his hand and strode out.

Sally slowly walked around the desk and sat down, hugging herself in excitement. She had made it! Here she was in Fleet Street, and an editor—well, Letters Editor—but still . . .

* * *

Sally's first flight into journalism didn't exactly hit the streets. That was not the way of *Home Chats*. It rather *filtered* its way into domestic homes and vicarages, where it mostly lay ignored until the cook took it away to the kitchen to copy the recipes, unaware that she had them already in her copy of Mrs. Beeton.

But first one person turned idly to the letter page and stared and showed it to another and another. Word of mouth is better than advertising any day, and soon copies of *Home Chats* were disappearing off the book stands and out of the kitchens as people exclaimed over Sally's advice.

It was her reply to the pregnant housemaid that caused the most furor. First of all, letter editors were not supposed to publish such letters. They were supposed to send vague, woolly replies in plain envelopes. But not only had Sally published it, but she had gone to town on her reply.

She had urged the fallen housemaid not to waste her time with unnecessary guilt. The child must come first. The father, if he were not in a position to marry the girl, must be made to pay child support. The man was just as responsible as the girl for the unborn child. Sally had urged the woman to ask her mistress for advice, since "no lady with a true Christian spirit would even consider turning you out of doors."

So those who were shocked at Sally's forthrightness felt hobbled when it came to writing a blistering reply, because nobody wanted to be accused of lacking in Christian spirit.

Then there was the girl who was being forced by her parents to marry the rich neighbor's son. "Don't do it," said Aunt Mabel—Sally.

> "Money cannot buy love, and there are times when one's parents do not know what is best for one. Honor thy father and thy mother—but by all means follow the dictates of your conscience."

Well, it was rather hard to argue with that one too.

By the time the next edition of *Home Chats* reached the public, the bewildered Mr. Barton found he had to increase the print, and Sally was in dire need of a secretary. Letters poured in by every post, and she worked long and hard to answer all of them. Then one night Mr. Barton had a brainstorm. He had never thought of that incredibly dull magazine ever blossoming into anything else. But why not? He, James Barton, could still be the reporter he had always longed to be. He knew he was good.

He walked out of the Red Lion, his pint of beer standing on the counter, untasted, and went back to the office and wrote a blistering article on the evils of prostitution. He had all the facts and figures at his fingertips, for he had written a free-lance article only the year before in a last-ditch attempt to prove himself. Now it would have a market.

In another month the big newspapers were beginning to sit up and take notice of this new child in their midst. Sally had an elderly secretary, a friend of Miss Fleming recruited from the lodging house, and two whole pages in the magazine. Mr. Barton had hired a reporter and spent the nights in consultation with his printer. The headlines became bolder and the stories stronger.

Following Sally's example, Mr. Barton qualified his most lurid stories by pointing out that they were just what every God-fearing, thinking man and woman should know about.

God, the Bible, and titillation was a heady mixture. The public lapped it up. They could read all those scandalous letters and stories and know that it was their Christian duty to read such things.

Sales soared, and so did Sally's salary. The dissolute relatives of the late Reverend Entwhistle became even more dissolute on the proceeds, and Mr. Barton could be seen drinking champagne occasionally in El Vino's instead of sipping bitters in the Red Lion.

Sally and her secretary, Miss Frimp, and Miss Fleming left the lodging house and took an apartment in Bloomsbury.

Sally forgot about Emily and the children. Her whole life was centered in that one cluttered room behind the frosted glass door. She worked long and late. She enjoyed the heady feeling of exhaustion, the smell of success, the feeling of a day's work well done, as she walked out into Fleet Street and looked down that famous canyon, breathing in the smell of hot paper, feeling the thud of the presses, and seeing the sooty dome of St. Paul's floating against the night sky.

She hardly thought of romance or love or marriage.

In fact, she was getting a peculiar insight into the pitfalls of love, romance, and marriage as anguished letter after anguished letter reached her desk.

But strangely enough no one ever tried to find out the identity of the now-famous Aunt Mabel. The little old lady with the spectacles still beamed out wisely from the top of the page.

No matter how much he imbibed in the hostelries of Fleet Street, Mr. Barton always referred carefully to Aunt Mabel as "a nice old girl."

And then one day the axe fell—in the form of a crested letter. Much impressed, Miss Frimp passed it over to Sally to open personally.

Sally read it through twice and then said faintly, "I must consult Mr. Barton."

That gentleman was happily engrossed in his latest exposé—"A Day in a London Slum"—when Sally walked in and handed him the letter silently.

He whistled between his teeth as he read.

It was more like a royal command than a letter. The Duchess of Dartware had written, requesting Aunt Mabel's presence at a house party in a week's time. The duchess said her son

51

was about to become affianced to a *most* unsuitable young girl, and she wished to have Aunt Mabel's advice.

Mr. Barton stared at it and then stopped whistling and looked up. "Well, you can't go, Miss Blane. Aunt Mabel *must* remain anonymous. Tell you what. I'll write to her nibs and tell her that you never go anywhere, but that if she supplies you with a few more details, you'll *write* the advice. That should fix her."

Sally sighed with relief and went back to bury herself in her work. But somewhere there was a nagging feeling of disappointment. It would have been marvelous to have been able to visit a ducal home . . . just once.

Mr. Barton sent the letter to the duchess, and the duchess replied by wire.

> Stop waffling stop send Aunt Mabel stop if you do not send Aunt Mabel I shall call at your office in person stop so don't be a silly twit stop
>
> Mary Duchess of Dartware

Sally and Mr. Barton stared at each other over the wire in consternation.

"We're sunk." said Mr. Barton, clutching his head.

"I have it," said Sally. "We'll let her call here. Miss Frimp can pretend to be me."

But Miss Frimp nearly fainted at the very idea. Normally a timid soul, she dug her heels in on this one occasion and refused to budge, which left them exactly where they were.

Mr. Barton scowled while Sally paced up and down the room. She stopped suddenly and stared at a theatrical poster on the wall, and a mischievous smile lit up her face.

"I've got it!" she exclaimed.

"What?" cried Mr. Barton, who truly believed Sally to be omnipotent.

"I'll hire a theatrical makeup artist," said Sally. "A white wig, some spectacles with plain glass, and some rubber wrinkles, and—*voilà!* Aunt Mabel."

"It'll never work," said Mr. Barton, but he looked longingly toward his unfinished article.

"Of course it will," said Sally bracingly. "Nothing to it! Two days with the old trout and I'll be back." She twitched the wire out of Mr. Barton's unresisting fingers. "I'll reply to this. Imagine! I'm going to be a duchess's guest!"

Her hope and happiness buoyed her up all the way back to Bloomsbury, but there she met with a setback as her two older flatmates digested the news.

Miss Frimp, released from the social confines of the office where Sally was her boss, flatly stated that she thought the whole idea was "terribly dangerous." Miss Fleming said gloomily that Sally was bound to be found out.

The three women were sitting drinking tea around the table of their sparsely furnished living room, which was devoid of the usual feminine knickknacks that one would expect three single ladies with good salaries to have.

But the fact was that all three worked long hours and never seemed to have the time to pay much attention to their home, short of paying a char to keep the place clean.

Sally had never regretted having chosen such odd flatmates instead of girls of her own age. She enjoyed Miss Fleming's tough, intelligent brain and inside-out knowledge of the workings of Fleet Street, and she enjoyed equally Miss Frimp's old-maidish manners and frequent shy little jokes.

They argued the pros and cons far into

night, and by bedtime, Sally was more than ever determined to go.

Miss Frimp, who looked so like that picture of Aunt Mabel in the magazine, said with her infectious feminine giggle, "What if you were to marry the duchess's son yourself?"

"He'll probably be some pimply adolescent who's fallen for a chorus girl," said Sally. "And don't forget, I shall be covered in rubber wrinkles."

"Hadn't you better look him up in *Debrett's Peerage*? volunteered Miss Fleming. "Might as well find out who he is."

"Time enough for that," said Sally, yawning. "All the time in the world . . ."

CHAPTER THREE

There has always been a lack of respect for titles and dignitaries in Fleet Street. A story is a story, whether it concerns Little Johnny Bloggs, age three, in Clapham, stuck down a coalhole—"He was ever so brave," said thirty-year-old brown-haired, blue-eyed Mrs. Mary Bloggs, laughingly, yesterday—or the latest goings-on of His Royal Highness, King Edward. Sally had acquired the Fleet Street outlook by a sort of osmosis, and therefore had not paused to really *think* about what being a guest of a duke and duchess would entail.

Admittedly the theatrical man had done a wonderful job, and even the anxious and critical Miss Frimp had failed to recognize Sally as the sweet little old lady who had emerged from under the hands of the expert.

Sally had bought most of her wardrobe at a sale for Indigent Gentlewomen, balking at spending much of her precious salary on this masquerade.

She was to travel by train to Bath, and there she would be met and conveyed to Banjahar Palace. Sally had still failed to look him up in *Debrett's* before leaving, and so had only a vague idea of the family she was going to meet.

The Dukedom of Dartware was pretty young by British standards. The first had gained his title in an obscure and undramatic way. With a handful of men, he had fought and overcome the small town of Banjahar in India, a place no one had heard of. He had also overcome the local nabob and had taken the man's fortune in jewels as a sort of military reward. The most magnificent of these, he had presented on his return to King George II, who had not heard of Banjahar, nor did he even know where it was, but his royal eye was delighted with the presents. The king had also been imbibing a little too freely, and so he had made Colonel John Daumaunt First Duke of Dartware, Dartware being the name of the village over which the Daumaunts had ruled since the Norman Conquest. The first duke had decreed a stately palace to be built, and to celebrate his "famous" victory, he named it Banjahar.

That brilliant soldier, Clive of India, Baron Clive of Plassey, certainly had been heard to mutter on frequent occasions that he had never even heard of Banjahar, and why had Daumaunt gone to war against the nabob when he and his regiment were supposed to be somewhere entirely different?

But for all his failings as a military man, the first duke had proved to be a brilliant farmer and had made good use of all the agricultural revolutions of the eighteenth century, trebling his original fortune.

Of all this history Sally was only a little aware. It was after she had alighted from the train at Bath that she got an inkling of what was in store for her.

The magnificence of the carriage that was to bear her to Banjahar made her blink. Its crested panels gleamed in the dusty sunlight filtering through the sooty glass of the station. The footmen in their powdered wigs were at least six and a half feet tall, and the coachman looked as grand as a duke himself.

The well-sprung carriage bowled out of Bath, and Sally began nervously to consider her position. Where would she eat, for example? With the family? With the servants? In the nursery with the governess? The day was very warm, and she sent up a silent prayer that her rubber wrinkles would not become unglued.

Her worries and anxieties prevented her from admiring the view, and she was not even aware that they had traveled quite a distance until the coachman on the box shouted *"Banjahar!"* As she leaned from the carriage window he pointed down into the valley with his whip.

Sally took one look and leaned back, her knees knocking in sudden fright. The valley of Dartware lay spread out below the ridge along which they were traveling. And set in the middle of the valley like some exotic gem lay Banjahar.

Built of mellow portland stone, the huge mass of Banjahar, with its many towers and courtyards and pinnacles, lay spread out in the sun. Behind the house the lake and the many ornamental trees that set it off were a beautiful example of the work of Capability Brown.

The carriage turned and rolled to a halt before two imposing gateposts topped with stone tigers lying on their backs with their paws in the air. This, as Sally was to learn later, was to symbolize the first duke's successful battle, but all her frightened mind could take in as the lodgekeeper ran to open the gates were idiocies such as *What on earth is the heraldic term for an animal in a stupid position like that? Rampant? No . . . that's standing up with paw raised like the lion of Scotland. Couchant? No, that's lying down. Oh, dear, I wish I hadn't come. It's like going to Buckingham Palace to play some awful joke.*

The carriage was now through the gates and bowling smoothly up a long, straight drive lined alternately with wellingtonias and statues of nude ladies with large hips, thick legs, and superior smiles on their faces. All too soon for Sally—although it was a very long drive indeed —the carriage was swinging around to stop at the main entrance under the shadow of an enormous statue of Pallas Athene on a pediment.

Sally, feeling as frail as the old lady she was supposed to be, allowed herself to be helped down from the carriage.

A small figure in black silk with a black straw

hat and black lace mittens, Sally slowly mounted the marble steps, flanked on either side by slain Indians—executed by Grinling Gibbons—and felt her heart sink somewhere down inside her elastic-sided boots.

I'm frightened to death, thought Sally.

"I'm frightened to death," said Her Grace, the Duchess of Dartware.

"Well, you asked the woman, darling," pointed out Mrs. Annabelle Stuart, a thin, acidulous lady. "You should have consulted me first. Fleet Street is packed wall to wall with grubby, encroaching people. I should know! When Jeremy —my cousin, you know—had that unfortunate affair with that chorus girl, they printed the whole thing all over the social page, carefully wrapped, tied, and delivered in genteel prose."

"Ugh!" The duchess fanned herself vigorously and stared around the room for support.

The duke and duchess and their houseguests were seated in the long drawing room, which took up quite a sizeable portion of the ground floor of the palace.

The ducal son, Paul, Marquess of Seudenham had gone out riding.

The houseguests were Miss Margery Wynd-ham, an aristocratic beauty who had been invit-ed by the marquess and to whom the duchess had taken a quite unreasonable dislike—hence the summons to Aunt Mabel; Lady Veronica Chelmsford, a faded beauty, and her thin, horsey husband, Sir Sydney Chelmsford; Peter Firkin, a friend of the marquess, famous for his good-naturedness and total lack of brain; and the aforementioned Mrs. Stuart and her husband, the Honorable Freddie, a thin middle-aged man with a white weak face, held together by an eye-glass.

They were all dotted about the huge room in various chairs and clutching various drinks. Conversation was by necessity full-throated, since it was like trying to carry on a chat with someone at the far end of a rugby pitch.

The duchess had just told them all about her invitation to Aunt Mabel and that she now re-gretted it.

"I don't see why you are frightened," said Peter Firkin with a puzzled look. "Old bird, ain't she. I mean to say, tells gels what to do about their lovelife, what. Anything the matter with your lovelife, Duchess? Haw, haw, haw!"

"Not mine," said the duchess, much flustered. "I don't want to tell you *why* I invited her, but I was at my wit's end, and it seemed the thing to do, but now I don't want this stranger here. She'll probably fix me with a gimlet eye and search out the secrets of my soul."

"Oh, I say," said Peter Firkin awkwardly, running a finger around his collar.

"Balderdash!" said Mrs. Stuart roundly. "Give her tea and send her packing."

The duchess moved her small, curved body restlessly on the chair. Everything about Her Grace was curved, from the droop of her eyelids to her thin-lipped mouth and well-upholstered body. She had heavy masses of pure white hair, which she wore fashionably dressed low on her forehead. It was the only remaining relic of her once considerable beauty.

The duke was unconcerned about his wife's forthcoming guest. He detested houseparties and slept through as much of them as possible. His head was hidden behind the *Times,* which rose and fell with each gentle snore.

"Too late," said Miss Wyndham with a light laugh. "I hear a carriage outside."

Everyone sat in silence, listening.

The double doors at the end of the room were thrown open, and the butler announced in a pained voice, "Aunt Mabel of *Home Chats.*"

Sally stood and blinked behind the plain glass of her gold-rimmed spectacles. The room seemed to stretch for miles and miles, punctuated at intervals by bodies with staring eyes.

The duchess gave a little sigh of relief. There was nothing at all intimidating about Aunt Mabel. From her white hair to her neat boots, she looked the picture of mild English spinsterhood. Her eyes, behind their barrier of spectacles, looked surprisingly youthful and candid. Apart from that, she was certainly amazingly old and wrinkled, and that reassured the duchess even more.

She bustled forward and took Aunt Mabel's mittened hands in her own. "So glad you have arrived, my dear. We will have a little chat. You must have some tea. I shall introduce you to everyone later. Ah, but you simply must meet Margery—Miss Wyndham. Margery, do come over and say hullo to Aunt Mabel."

Sally turned slightly. A vision in blond lace was gliding toward her. Margery Wyndham was twenty-one and looked somewhat older because of her poise and classic beauty. She had heavy fair hair, caught in a thick coil at the back of her neck.

Her complexion was flawless and her expression sweet. She had large, well-shaped blue eyes. Her tea gown must have cost a small fortune in priceless lace, and the heavy rope of pearls around her neck reached to her knees.

She murmured a conventional greeting, and then Sally was borne off by the duchess. "We will go into the morning room," said that lady, "for now that we have met I cannot wait to unburden myself. I am a great admirer of your column. So sensible! So forthright! I am sure you will be able to tell me exactly what to do."

The duchess's rather high, penetrating voice echoed around the marble entrance hall as she led Sally across it.

I should possibly develop a penetrating voice myself, thought Sally, *if I lived in these gigantic rooms.*

The morning room, which was at the end of a chain of passages, was reassuringly small. Its French windows were open to a view of the ornamental lake at the back of the house, and the sunlight sent water patterns wavering over the pretty gilt furniture and brocade curtains.

The occasional tables and mantelshelf were crammed with priceless porcelain. A coy tiger by Johann Gottlieb Kirchner leered up at Sally with its white porcelain eyes, and an indiscreet harlequin by Kaendler clutched the china bosom of his Columbine with frivolous unconcern.

Two maids in long white starched aprons and frilly lace caps entered silently and set the tea things on a round marble table.

Sally began to relax. The duchess was not formidable after all. The palace *was* rather overpowering, but with luck she would not have to stay for long. She settled back while the duchess dismissed the maids and busied herself among the teacups. To Sally's amazement the duchess proved to be a "miffer." The miffers, as any good etiquette book will tell you, are those socially unacceptable women who put the milk in first when serving tea—the milk-in-firsts. But she assumed after some hard thought that duchesses, being born at the very top of the social tree, did not have to labor over etiquette books.

Sally wondered if she should remove her mittens. She knew—etiquette books again—that one was supposed to keep one's gloves on except when eating bread and butter, and there was no bread and butter, only cucumber sandwiches, seedcake, plum cake, and scones.

But the duchess's opening remarks drove all thoughts of etiquette from Sally's mind.

"Now," began Her Grace, after slurping tea with all the elegance of a coal heaver, "my problem concerns my little boy, Paul. Of course, he's not little anymore, being quite grown up. He has become enamored of that Margery girl. And it won't *do*."

"Perhaps she is a trifle old for him," ventured Sally in her quavery Aunt Mabel voice.

"Not at all," said the duchess in a forthright manner, spreading seedcake liberally with jam and butter before stuffing it in her mouth.

Sally took the opportunity to eat a cucumber sandwich herself while her mind worked furiously. She glanced around quickly and then out of the French windows, where the formal gardens ran down to the lakeside. It must cost a fortune to run a place like this. That must be it! Miss Wyndham did not have money.

"Is Miss Wyndham . . . er . . . not very rich?" suggested Sally.

"Oh, yes, I mean, she is," said the duchess. "Pots and pots."

"Perhaps she is mean and unkind?"

"Sweet and thoughtful."

"Well, then," said Sally, beginning to feel exasperated, "you had better tell me why you don't like Miss Wyndham."

"She's too good for him . . . Paul . . . my son."

Sally looked wise while her brain seemed to consist of nothing more than a row of question marks. The most she could hope for was that the duchess would *explain*.

"You see," went on Her Grace, "she would *bore* Paul. He's always liked women with a bit of vice in them. Goodness knows, he's kept a stable of them."

Sally was beginning to feel completely out of her depth. At first she had thought of Paul as a pimply young adolescent, now she decided he must be a young rake. Probably one of those young men who were sent down from Oxford and who settled down to making their parents' lives as uncomfortable as possible.

Stable of women indeed! The silly boy was probably trying just to alarm his mother.

"You must be tired," said the duchess sympathetically. "Paul is having dinner with friends this evening and will not be back until late. If you could perhaps see him then? Say you had a little nap now?"

Sally nodded, all at once glad of a chance to escape. Her skin was itching under its coat of rubber wrinkles, the unaccustomed spectacles felt heavy on her nose, and her wig felt hot and heavy. She felt very young and rather scared.

The duchess, to Sally's relief, began to discuss fashions while Sally finished her tea. What did Sally think of the latest Nell Gwyn hat, the Camille Clifford coiffure, the Billie Burke shoe, and the Trilby overcoat? Sally murmured innocuous remarks between bites and then took refuge in her supposed age, saying she was too old to keep up with the modes. In fact, she had been too busy being simply Aunt Mabel since her arrival in London that the world of fashion had passed her by.

All of a sudden Sally found herself thinking of Miss Wyndham's tea gown. It must be simply marvelous to wear something like that.

At last she was free to retire. A servant conducted her to her room, which was in fact more of a young apartment, boasting a sitting room and bathroom as well as a bedroom.

The lace curtains at the windows floated in a light breeze. Down below, a swan cruised majestically over the watered silk of the lake.

Sally undressed and took off her heavy whalebone corsets and gave herself a good scratch, which was what she had been longing to do since she left London.

At first she did not want to lie down at all, but the bedroom looked very cool with its blinds pulled down and the bed itself tempting with its pretty white lace canopy. A pile of French novels, their pages uncut, lay on a table beside the bed.

She lay down on the bed and picked up one of the novels and stared at it, unseeing. Suddenly the effort of reaching for the paper knife and cutting the pages seemed too much, and in no time at all she was fast asleep.

Sally awoke with a guilty start just as the dressing gong rang somewhere in the great house. She scrambled from the bed to find that a maid had entered while she was asleep and had carefully taken away her dinner gown, had it pressed, and laid it out.

Well, it was a bit hard to put on frumpish lilac silk of an antique cut, ornamented with swirls of jet embroidery, and step back into that pouter pigeon corset. It would have been so splendid to have worn something really pretty and to have gone as herself.

Dinner was a surprising affair. In the first place, the food was remarkably pedestrian, considering this was a ducal mansion and this the heyday of the gourmet. It reminded Sally forcibly of her nursery days as she worked her way through courses consisting of such delights as stewed mutton, watery cabbage, boiled potatoes, shriveled smelts, and treacle pudding.

Across the table from Sally, Miss Margery Wyndham blazed in all her glory. Her beauty was almost luminous, decided Sally, and her large, expressive eyes were shining with dreams.

I believe she is in love, thought Sally. *Drat it! If the duchess's son wants her, then I can't see her refusing him.*

Miss Wyndham was dressed in apricot silk, cut low to reveal an excellent pair of white shoulders. Her hair that evening was fashionably dressed and frizzed and threaded with apricot silk roses.

Sally was flanked on one side by Peter Firkin and on the other by Sir Sydney Chelmsford. Sir Sydney was a taciturn gentleman who gave his whole attention to his food. Peter Firkin addressed a few almost unintelligible remarks to Sally and then devoted his attention to Mrs. Stuart, who was placed on his other side.

She soon lost interest in the general conversation, which concerned people she did not know and had never heard of. Sally studied the room instead. Its walls were decorated with delicately painted panels, and Sally's wandering eyes rested on one of them, and then she felt herself begin to blush.

It was a peculiarly graphic portrayal of the Rape of Lucrece. Lucrece's large bosom spilled over the tanned and ravishing hands of Sextus, son of Tarquinius Superbus.

Sally hurriedly averted her eyes and stared at another panel. In it Iphigeneia was dying in all her voluptuous naked glory, sacrificed at the altar to Artemis, so that the Greek ships should have a fair wind to the Trojan war.

So she stared at her plate instead.

She wondered what the Watch Committee

would make of it all. But then art and antiquity excused all.

"Jolly good that, what?" said Peter Firkin suddenly, pointing with his fork at the sacrifice of Iphigeneia. "Jolly ships, what? Look as if they could sail right out of the picture, don't you know, eh, what?"

"It is a very bold subject," said Sally in her most repressive Aunt Mabelish voice.

"Eh, what?" Peter stared blankly at the picture. "Oh, yes, haw, haw, haw. Hot stuff!" He let out a great bray of laughter, turned beet red, and buried his nose in his wineglass.

He's rather old to be a friend to Paul, thought Sally, observing him out of the corner of her eye with some irritation. She began to wonder about her forthcoming interview. She wondered what this rakehell young man would make of having Aunt Mabel brought in to advise him against marriage to the beautiful Miss Wyndham.

And how could she possibly put it into words? As the duchess had done? Miss Wyndham is too good for you?

All too soon the ladies rose to leave the gentlemen to their port. The duchess immediately drew Sally aside. "Come with me," she whispered. "Paul is home. I will have him sent to you."

With a rapidly beating heart, Sally followed the duchess back through a bewildering array of rooms and found herself in an enormous library, which looked down the drive at the front of the palace.

It smelled slightly of leather, potpourri, and stale tobacco. Serried ranks of books mounted up to the painted ceiling. Sally quickly lowered her eyes from the ceiling. Goodness knew what might be up there getting raped or sacrificed.

A footman came in silently after them and set a decanter of whisky and a soda siphon on a low table near the windows, which were flanked by two high-backed easy chairs.

"Now," said the duchess, with a surprisingly girlish giggle, "I will send my bad boy along. Won't he be surprised!"

"But doesn't he know . . . ?" began Sally desperately, but the duchess had fluttered off.

Sally clasped her hands together. Outside on the terrace a peacock strutted past silently. A faint smell of thyme drifted in from the gardens.

What shall I say to him? wondered Sally. *Her Grace has planned this as a surprise. He'll prob-*

ably sneer most dreadfully. And what rank does a duke's only son hold anyway? Marquess, I think.

The door opened, and Sally remained where she was, quite still, seated in one of the armchairs beside the long windows looking out into the darkness of the gardens.

"Surprise!" came the duchess's voice from the door. "Paul, darling, this is Aunt Mabel of *Home Chats.* Aunt Mabel, my son, Paul, Marquess of Scudenham. I'll leave you two together!"

Sally tried to struggle to her feet, but a deep voice said, "Please, don't. I shall join you."

Resplendent in black-and-white evening dress, the Marquess of Seudenham sank into the armchair opposite.

Sally gazed at him, unbelieving. He was the handsomest man she had ever seen, from his thick black hair to his bright, mocking blue eyes, set in a tanned face, to his lithe, muscular body. And he was no adolescent. She judged him to be in his middle thirties.

The marquess looked curiously at the little old lady who was staring at him so intently. Her face looked rather stiff and odd, he thought, and she was very wrinkled indeed. Only her large gray eyes seemed to be alive. He helped himself to a whisky and soda, frowning as he realized no other refreshment had been set out suitable to an old lady like Aunt Mabel.

He waited for her to speak, but she was still gazing at him helplessly, so he said, "Aunt . . . er . . . Mabel? Which side of the family?"

"*Home Chats*," croaked Sally.

"*Home* . . . ? Oh, no! You're not one of those ladies who give advice to the lovelorn?"

"Yes," mumbled Sally, suddenly helping herself to a whisky and soda.

"Mama has really gone too far this time . . . er . . . Aunt Mabel. Who am I supposed to be lovelorn over?"

"Miss Wyndham."

"Really? My mother knows more about it than I do. Does she want me to marry the girl?"

Sally took a large gulp of her drink and looked at him shyly. "The duchess doesn't want you to marry her at all."

"Your words surprise me. Miss Wyndham is young and beautiful and rich. All the things to gladden a mother's heart. What's up with her?"

"Nothing," said Sally weakly and then again,

"*Nothing,*" in a stronger voice as she gathered the mantle of Aunt Mabel about her. "Your mother thinks she is too good for you. Her Grace thinks you need a lady with a little more vice in her."

He put down his glass and leaned back in his chair and laughed loud and long while Sally stared at him with adoring eyes.

At last he finished laughing, and Sally adjusted her expression to one—she hoped—of rather prim wisdom.

"And so the decision, I gather, is to be left to you? I think that must be why Mama sprang this surprise on me."

"I should think so," quavered Sally, very much Aunt Mabel.

"What *is* your decision?"

Sally bent her head and appeared to concentrate. Actually she had made a lightning decision. This handsome marquess should really marry no one else but Miss Sally Blane. How it was to be achieved, she could not even begin to imagine. But she had wanted to work on Fleet Street—and she did. All things were possible if the modern Edwardian career woman put her mind to it.

"I think you should only marry for love," she said.

He raised his eyebrows. "And what makes you think I am not in love with Miss Wyndham?"

"You are too detached," said Sally.

"Love, in my opinion," said the marquess, "is only a fleeting fancy. I am heading rapidly for middle age. I am thirty-five years old, which must not seem much to you"—Sally winced—"nonetheless, it is time I settled down."

"Have you never been in love?" asked Sally curiously.

"Oh, hundreds of times." He paused, momentarily taken aback by the strange look of pain in the expressive eyes of the old lady opposite, who was now gulping her whisky as if it were water. "It never lasted. Can I get you another drink? Perhaps something milder? Sherry, perhaps?"

"No," said Aunt Mabel grimly, "whisky will do very well." Made bold by the spirit, she addressed him earnestly. "My dear lord, I have had great experience in matters of the heart. If you marry some girl simply because you think she will make a suitable wife, then your marriage will be doomed from the start. And then think of the children—the sticky, jammy, screaming, *awful* children," said Sally with sudden drunken fervor, thinking of Emily's noisy brood.

He crossed one elegantly tailored leg over the other and leaned back in his chair. Sally studied his handsome profile in the lamplight and sighed.

"I am beginning to think you do not approve of marriage at all," he said. "Are you, or have you been, married yourself?"

"No, my lord."

"In that case—"

"But I must assure you, as a detached observer, I have great insight into the problems of matrimony," said Sally.

He looked at her curiously. It was almost as if, by some trick of the light, a young and beautiful and intense girl were superimposed like a phantom over the wrinkled and aged features of Aunt Mabel.

Then he noticed that the hand holding her glass was trembling slightly and gently took the drink from her and put it on the table.

"We will discuss this further tomorrow," he said, getting to his feet. "I think you should rest. It is very late."

Sally allowed him to help her to her feet.

"Would you assist me to my room?" she quavered. "I do feel shaky." And in truth, she did, not being used to hard liquor.

Ah! The benefits of being old, thought Sally as the marquess put one strong arm around her. She leaned against him gratefully and moved as slowly as possible so as to prolong this delicious experience.

He felt the old lady tremble slightly and experienced a qualm of anxiety. She was a queer old bird, and it was certainly long past her bedtime.

He escorted her to the door of her sitting room and politely held the door open for her, receiving a blazing look from a pair of glowing eyes.

Naughty old thing, thought the marquess, much amused. *I believe she's got a crush on me.*

CHAPTER FOUR

Sally carefully sponged her rubber wrinkles in the morning, wishing heartily that she could tear the whole mess from her face. But the role of Aunt Mabel had to be kept up, the pouter pigeon corset to be struggled into, and the stuffy, hot old ladies' clothes to be put on.

It was going to be another very long day.

She drank her tea—brought in by the maid— and ate her Osborne biscuits and found that her stomach was still rumbling, and so she went in search of the breakfast room, eventually being guided to it by a footman.

It transpired that everyone else, with the exception of Peter Firkin, was breakfasting in their rooms. Sally helped herself to a generous portion of bacon and grilled kidneys from the enormous array of dishes on the sideboard and sat down primly opposite Mr. Firkin, whose nose was buried in the morning paper.

She hoped he would not trouble to engage her in conversation, but no sooner had she begun to eat than she became aware of one large hazel eye surveying her over the top of the newspaper.

"Aunt Mabel?"

Sally put down her knife and fork with a little sigh. "Yes, Mr. Firkin?"

"I say, do you give chappies advice as well as the gels?"

"Oh, yes, especially after I have eaten something and woken up properly," said Sally repressively.

"Haw, jolly good," said Mr. Firkin, throwing aside the newspaper so that it fell across the marmalade. "Fact is, I'm awfully much in need of someone to natter to about *things*."

Sally sighed. "Natter away, Mr. Firkin," she said.

"Well, haw, haw, it's jolly awkward getting it out, 'specially as I've always been one of the strong, silent types, don't you know, eh what, haw. Fact is . . . I'm in love." And with that admission Mr. Firkin blushed like a schoolboy and buried his nose in his coffee cup.

Sally surveyed him with some amusement, took several hasty bites of her breakfast, and urged, "Do go on."

"Don't know how to begin," said Mr. Firkin, throwing himself back in his chair, crossing his legs, and swinging one foot so that it smacked up against the underside of the table, sending a small wave of Sally's tea cascading over her breakfast plate.

"Try," said Sally, resolving to try to eat breakfast when Mr. Firkin was in a less energetic state.

"It'slikethis," he said in a rush. "I'm most awfully, frightfully, *terribly* smitten with Miss Wyndham."

Lovely Mr. Firkin! Brave Mr. Firkin! Splendid Mr. Firkin!

"And she's in love with you," said Sally, smiling.

"Oh, no. I think she's in love with Paul."

Stupid, dreary, *useless* Mr. Firkin.

"Are you *sure*?"

"Well, stands to reason. He's got the title, he's

terribly rich, he's handsome. Any gel would pre-
fer him to me."

"Oh, *yes*," breathed Sally dreamily, and then
caught his huffy look of surprise.

"No, no, I don't mean that," she said hurriedly. "I mean one would think so. On the other
hand"—Sally crossed her fingers behind her
back—"you are a remarkably good-looking
young man. Yes, I would say you are definitely
what I would call attractive."

Peter Firkin blushed and looked at her ador-
ingly.

"It is necessary," went on Sally cautiously,
"to take some action. It is no use sitting around
inarticulate. You must have courage! You must
woo her. And you must tell his lordship, the
marquess, that your feelings are engaged, so that
he will not come between you and Miss Wyndham. I happen to know that his lordship is indifferent to Miss Wyndham."

"I say, you can't go around saying things like
that to another chappie when the chappie's your
friend! And Paul . . . well, he can be a funny sort
of cove. He might laugh—and—and I don't
think I could *bear* that."

"I shall speak to him if you like," volunteered Sally, completely forgetting about breakfast.

"Oh, *would* you? I say, Aunt Mabel, you are absolutely the cat's pajamas. If I were younger, I'd marry you instead."

"Oh, Mr. Firkin," said Sally roguishly. "You *naughty* man."

And absolutely delighted with each other, the pair finished their breakfasts.

Sally felt quite powerful and elated. Being Aunt Mabel certainly had its advantages.

But it was not until late in the day that Sally had her much longed-for talk with the marquess. First, directly after breakfast, she had been accosted by the housekeeper, a formidable lady, all bosom and no hips, who wanted to seek Aunt Mabel's advice on the insobriety of the butler and the peccadilloes of the footmen.

Luncheon was a dreary affair for Sally, since the marquess was seated next to Miss Wyndham and seemed to be flirting outrageously. Then, after luncheon, Her Grace wished a report on Aunt Mabel's talk with her son. Then, because of her great age, Sally was almost forced to lie down in the afternoon while "the young people" —everyone under sixty—went out for a drive.

As the duchess was leaving Aunt Mabel in her sitting room, she turned at the door and said, "I have a simply marvelous idea. Paul obviously wants just to get married. Therefore it is up to us to find him someone suitable! I shall give a ball and invite all the prettiest and raciest girls."

Sally longed to cry out, "Oh, don't do that!" but Aunt Mabel said instead, "A very good idea."

The duchess tilted her head to one side and surveyed Aunt Mabel. "You know, I think it was such a good idea getting you here. You must come for the ball. Simply must attend. What fun we will have watching to see which one Paul chooses!"

"Yes," said Sally bleakly. "On the other hand, I must really return to London. You see, I have many letters to—"

"Of course you have!" said the duchess blithely, "and I took the liberty of telephoning that Mr. Barton and telling him to forward all your mail here. He wanted to send your secretary, but I said there was no need for that. You can use mine. Have you met him? He's cataloging the library just now. Mr. Worthing. So *that's* all right. You will be here for the ball. Now, please lie down, dear, and rest your old bones, and we shall see you at dinner."

The duchess went off merrily, and Sally slumped miserably in her chair. She did not want to sleep. She wanted simply to go to that ball as anyone other than Aunt Mabel.

It was with something of a feeling of relief that Sally welcomed the arrival of two sacks of mail that had arrived by train that morning and had been collected by the duke's servants.

She debated whether to go down to the library and engage the services of the duke's secretary, but then decided to work on the letters herself. All at once she wanted to keep thoughts of the marquess out of her mind.

I must be terribly kind to old people, thought Sally as she settled down to her work. *How awful to be excluded from everything.*

She worked away steadily until a maid arrived at six o'clock with the news that the marquess wished to have a word with her.

With a rapidly beating heart, Sally adjusted her wig, patted her rubber wrinkles, and followed the maid to the long gallery on the first floor, where the marquess was sitting reading a copy of *Home Chats,* surrounded by the portraits of his ancestors.

He looked up at Sally and smiled in such a way that she felt quite breathless.

"Well, my wise Aunt Mabel," he said, rising and pulling a chair forward for her. "Have you come to a decision? Am I to offer my heart and my hand to Miss Wyndham?"

"I don't think you should," said Sally, carefully aging her voice. "Apart from the fact that you are not in love with Miss Wyndham, someone else is."

"Who?"

"Peter Firkin."

"Pull the other one," he said rudely. "I mean to say, *Peter.* I'm very fond of the old boy, and I've known him since we were at school together. But honestly, you must be mistaken. Peter *runs* from anything in a skirt, no matter what age. What on earth gave you that strange idea?"

"He told me."

"Good heavens! You are good at your job, if winkling dark secrets out of people is part of it. I must tease old Peter about this. Goodness, what a laugh!"

"The reason I am telling you this and not Mr.

Firkin," said Sally primly, "is because Mr. Firkin is very much in love and did not want to tell you just in case you *did* laugh at him."

"Dear me!" He raised his thin eyebrows. "I shall not embarrass him in any way. Actually, Peter is not dim at all. He was very bright at school, and under all that shyness lurks a pretty good brain. Ah, well . . . have you heard about mother's ball? She is importing suitable young ladies for my amusement. I wonder what has come over her. She never bothered before."

"Perhaps the duchess thinks it is time you settled down," said Sally.

"Undoubtedly. Never mind, I shall dance with you, Aunt Mabel, if you will save one for me."

Sally smiled bleakly. Then she looked around the long gallery. Was she aiming too high? The only money she had was what she had earned, apart from the two hundred pounds she had taken out of the bank in Lewes.

The aristocracy—particularly these days—did not lightly marry girls of a lower class with insignificant dowries.

She became aware that he was speaking again. "After all," he was saying in a light, mocking voice, "you quite put me off the whole idea. I hadn't thought of all those squalling brats running around the place."

"I was thinking of my sister's children," said Sally hurriedly. "Very spoiled, all of them."

"Your sister's children? Surely they are grown-up by now?"

"Oh, yes, *of course*. I was thinking of what they were like when they were little. But—but—all children need not be like that."

"No, no!" He laughed. "You have talked me out of it. Well, I must get changed for dinner." He hesitated before he had moved away a few paces. "I know little of Fleet Street, Aunt Mabel," he said, "but I must think it's very enterprising in a lady of your years to take on such a demanding job."

"I enjoy it," said Sally truthfully. "I learn a lot about myself from other people's problems. There is an infinite capacity in all of us for being wicked."

" 'The only original sin is opportunity,' " he quoted.

"Exactly. Given a different upbringing, say in Seven Dials, I, perhaps, would be capable of all the seven deadly sins at once."

"Tut-tut!" he mocked. "What a shocking old thing you are, to be sure. Are you leaving with me?"

"No, my lord. It is peaceful here. I shall sit and think of my sins."

"They can't be very many."

"Few," admitted Sally, "but quite colorful for all that." She turned a glowing pair of eyes on him, and then found he was watching her strangely, and she hurriedly looked down at her hands. When she looked up again he had gone.

Sally sat on in the long gallery, trying to still the turmoil of her soul. But she was not to be left in peace for long.

The door opened, and Miss Wyndham drifted into the room, a vision in a white lace tea gown threaded with rose silk ribbons. She was carrying a red hothouse rose in her hand.

"Isn't it pretty?" said Miss Wyndham with a dreamy smile on her beautiful face. "Paul gave it to me."

Oh, burning acid of jealousy! Sally felt cast adrift on a bright green sea of churning emotion.

"I wish to speak to you," went on Miss Wyndham, sinking into the chair recently vacated by *him*.

Bad etiquette, thought Sally sourly, feeling more like a bitter old spinster by the minute. *A lady is not supposed to sit in any seat warm from a gentleman's bottom.*

"I believe you are very sympathetic. I feel you have a clear and kind *soul.*" Miss Wyndham smiled beatifically into Sally's hate-filled eyes.

"How can I be of assistance?" asked Sally in a crotchety voice.

"I am in love," said Miss Wyndham simply, twisting the stem of the rose in her long white fingers.

"You *would* be!"

"I beg your pardon?" Miss Wyndham raised slightly startled eyes.

"I said, I thought you were," lied Sally, sternly, and with stupendous effort banishing jealousy into the far corner of her heart.

"Oh, does it show?" She blushed prettily. "The trouble is that I don't think he even notices me. Do you think he is shy?"

Sally thought longingly of the marquess. "No," she said. "I would not have thought that at all."

Miss Wyndham looked sad. "You must be right, because you are so wise. Then it must be that he does not care for me. I only accepted the invitation so as to be near him. Do you think I have any hope?''

Sally looked at the beautiful girl opposite. "Perhaps," she said slowly. "Why don't you wait until the ball? It will be a romantic atmosphere. Perhaps then you could summon up enough courage to give him a little encouragement." *Just give me time to think,* cried Sally's treacherous inner voice. "There are other young men who must find you very attractive." she added hopefully.

"I am not interested in any other young men," said Miss Wyndham, with infuriating simplicity. "Perhaps," she said, looking eagerly at Sally, "you yourself could mention some little thing."

"I'll try," replied Sally, wrestling with her conscience.

"You're a dear," said Miss Wyndham, getting to her feet and kissing Sally impulsively on the cheek. She looked rather startled as her lips came into contact with the cold rubber wrinkles on Sally's face.

When she had left, Sally sat chiding herself for her own jealousy and misery. How could she compete with a girl like Miss Wyndham, even supposing she were not disguised as Aunt Mabel? *But I would like to try,* screamed her rebellious inner voice. *If only I could go to that ball as myself.*

"You, there . . . er . . . Aunt Mabel, or whatever your name is," said an acid voice in her ear.

Sally stared upward into the cold eyes of Mrs. Annabelle Stuart. She struggled politely to her feet and found herself thrust back down into the chair with a strong hand.

"Sit down," commanded Mrs. Stuart. "You need all the rest you can get at your age."

She plumped herself down opposite and glared at Sally.

"Can I be of assistance?" asked Sally politely.

"I didn't come here to ask for help from some grubby little magazine's letters editor," barked Mrs. Stuart, and then relapsed into smoldering silence.

Sally raised her false eyebrows and did not deign to reply. At last she got to her feet and tried to make her escape.

"And where do you think you're going?" demanded Mrs. Stuart.

"To change for dinner."

"Time enough for that," snapped Mrs. Stuart,

and relapsed into a sort of brooding silence that was somehow familiar to Sally.

Then Sally realized Mrs. Stuart was sulking. "I am not a servant, Mrs. Stuart," said Sally at last with a faint edge to her voice. "My time is my own to spend as I see fit. So . . ." She got to her feet.

"Oh, if you must know, I *do* want your help," grumped Mrs. Stuart, playing with a hideous string of hand-thrown pottery beads that, in Sally's opinion, someone had not thrown far enough. They were those multicolored lumps in shades of sulphur-yellow and purple strung on black cord.

Sally gave a little sigh of resignation. "Please, go on," she said, adopting her Aunt Mabel expression of patient wisdom.

"I want to kill my husband, Freddie," said Mrs. Stuart.

"Why?" asked Sally in amazement.

"You really are rather a stupid old woman," said Mrs. Stuart nastily. "Anyone with half a brain would want to kill Freddie. He's a dead bore. He picks his teeth. He leaves the top off the tooth powder. He smokes cheroots in bed. He pinches housemaid's bottoms. Do you need anything else?"

"But you must have loved him," protested Sally.

"No. Who told you that?"

"Well, I mean, you married him."

"Oh, for Heaven's sake. You *are* naive. I married him for his money, like any other sensible girl of my generation. I don't want a divorce. Too messy. Detectives and Brighton hotels. Ugh! So I've decided to kill him. That's where you come in. You can tell me how to do it."

Sally sat in stunned silence. Purple shadows crept across the room. Somewhere outside, a rising wind began to moan in the trees, crying out the end of a long Indian summer and heralding the first bite of winter.

"Come on. Think, woman!" said Mrs. Stuart while those awful beads went *clunk, clunk, clunk.* "I'm asking you cos I've got to discuss it with someone, and you're honor bound not to mention it to a soul—just like a priest."

If I thought you were serious, you horrible frump, thought Sally, *then I would call the local police station. But I happen to have guessed that*

*this is some kind of spiteful joke. But I'll play
your little game.*

"Give me time," said Sally aloud, "to concentrate."

Mrs. Stuart waited with ill-concealed impa-
tience while Sally furrowed her rubber wrinkles
and thought hard. Now, Sally was a great fan of
the Sherlock Holmes stories and had also read a
great number of penny dreadful mysteries when
she was at school.

"What is Her Grace's doctor like?" asked
Sally at last. "I mean the one who would be
called in if anything happened?"

"Oh, old Barchester. He's senile. I don't know
why Mary and Hugh will insist on having him."
With difficulty, Sally identified Mary as the
duchess and Hugh as the duke.

"You mean he could be tricked?"

Mrs. Stuart looked at Sally with a gleam of
comprehension beginning to dawn in her pale
eyes. "Old Barchester doesn't know his arse
from his elbow," she said with simple venom.

Sally reflected briefly on the foul language of
the ladies of the county who could be heard
baying obscenities that would make a sailor
blush on the hunting field.

"Then that is your answer," said Sally coldly, since she thought this joke in very poor taste. "You simply put it about that your husband has a dickey heart and put some rat poison in his tea, or whatever, and there you are. Doctor Barchester will simply take your word for it."

"By George!" breathed Mrs. Stuart. "You're everything you're cracked up to be. I'll start this evening."

With that she strode from the room, crashing the door behind her. *Silly old cow,* thought Sally. *Someone should put rat poison in her tea. Let me get out of here before someone else—Oh, Lor'.*

The door opened, and His Grace, the Duke of Dartware, sidled in.

"Well, well, well, well," he said breezily, rubbing his hands. "All in the dark, what? Better light the lamps, eh, what?"

He lit a heavy brass oil lamp that was standing on the inlaid top of a handsome loo table next to Sally.

Sally shivered slightly, for the room had become very cold. Surely the duke didn't want her advice. Surely . . .

"I need your help, old girl," said His Grace, putting a red and wrinkled hand on Sally's knee.

He was a gray-haired, fresh-faced man in his sixties, with bushy gray eyebrows and a toothbrush mustache and a button of a nose. He bared his teeth in a nicotine-and-Old-Gold-coated smile.

Sally gave him her most charming smile. With just a bit of luck he would soon be her father-in-law. "How can I be of assistance?" she asked.

"Well, you see, as a matter of fact, dash it all, well it's like this. Oh, don't you know, to tell the truth . . . I'm in love!"

With that the duke released Sally's knee from a surprisingly powerful clutch and sat back, looking at her as apprehensively as a schoolboy with his hand caught in the biscuit barrel.

"Oh, dear," said Sally sedately. She was, she had felt, inured to shock by now. But who was the duke in love with? Mrs. Stuart? Lady Veronica Chelmsford?

"Who is this lady?" she asked.

"Rose Higgins," breathed the duke, his eyes bulging slightly.

Sally frowned. "She is not one of your guests?"

"No," said the duke. "Rose is the barmaid down at the Feathers in the village. You should see her drawing a pint of beer. There's a light just above the tap, and it shines on the muscles of her forearms in such a way, don't you know, makes a chap feel quite weak."

"Perhaps it's just a passing fancy," suggested Sally hopefully. "How long have you known Miss Higgins?"

"Two years," said the duke gloomily.

"And she is aware of your feelings?"

The duke looked scandalized. "Of course not! I'm a gentleman. Wouldn't make approaches to a lady like that unless I were in a position to marry her."

"Marry! . . . Oh, dear. You cannot possibly marry her."

"Don't see why not," said the duke sulkily. "Divorce is a bit more common these days. Nobody minds. Won't let you into the Royal Enclosure at Ascot, but apart from that, nobody cares."

Sally took a deep breath. Her loyalty was to the duchess. The marquess, furthermore, would surely be distressed if his parents divorced.

"My dear duke," she said firmly. "I cannot approve . . ."

"Thought you would say that . . ."

"*Cannot* approve. Think of your son!"

"Paul!" exclaimed the duke huffily. "He's a masher of the first water. Fillies all over the place. At least *my* intentions are honorable! Look here, Aunt Mabel. There's a lovely little garden at the back of the Feathers. I know it's a bit cold this time of year, but perhaps you could drive there with me tomorrow, just to meet Rose. Now you'd do that, wouldn't you?"

"Yes," said Sally, more because she wanted to end this embarrassing conversation than to oblige her host.

"Splendid! Two o'clock, shall we say? Good!" And with that he left.

Dinner was a most embarrassing affair for poor Sally, who felt quite weighed down with all the dark secrets reposing in her jet-covered bosom. It was not as if she had to make any effort to converse with anyone at the table, because each and every one seemed to be speaking about exactly what was troubling them at the moment without any regard to their fellows.

"Freddie has got a dickey heart. Did you know?" Mrs. Stuart.

"I don't know where they get their cook from. Food's filth." The Honorable Freddie Stuart.

"I say, Miss Wyndham's in full bloom tonight, eh, what, haw? Makes the old ticker beat faster, what, haw!" Peter Firkin.

"A rose by any other name . . . Ah, Rose, Rose . . ." The duke.

". . . hope it will not be too much work for the servants. Perhaps I should get that chappie Marjie Effingham had to do her ballroom. Chinese, it was. Lengths of brocade and chrysanthemums in pots. So pretty . . ." The duchess.

"Servants are not trained properly these days and so uppity. All this Bolshevism." Lady Veronica Chelmsford.

"If only people *knew* what little me was thinking." Miss Wyndham.

"I say, I'll have second helpings, since you lot don't seem to like your food. Disgraceful waste. If you chaps had been in the army like me . . ." Sir Sydney Chelmsford.

"For the *fourth* time, I'm driving into Bath tomorrow, if anyone wants to go." The Marquess of Seudenham.

"Oh, I would love to go." Sally.

Both turned slightly and looked at each other

while the other voices rose and fell in their various monologues.

Then Sally's face fell. "I can't." she said dismally, forgetting to use her Aunt Mabel voice. "The duke is taking me to the village pub."

"Really?" said the marquess, looking amused. "Is that *still* going on?"

"What?" said Sally cautiously.

"That barmaid, whatsername?"

"Rose, Oh, you *know*!"

"Course I do. So does Mother. But what on earth is Father thinking of to trot a lady like you into barrooms?"

"We're going to sit in the garden."

"You'll freeze. Furthermore, you can't study the beauty of Rose's forearms from the garden."

"You are all quite mad," said Sally repressively. "I took the duke's confidence very seriously indeed. Particularly as he said he wanted to marry the girl."

"Don't worry your white hairs over it," said the marquess lazily. "Father's always been going to marry 'em over the years. Mother's quite happy that this current one is safely tucked away in the Feathers and not housed in the servants' hall, as is usually the case."

"Then I am wasting my time," said Sally sadly, for she wanted naturally to be free to go into Bath with the marquess.

He eyed her sympathetically. "It's all a bit much for you, isn't it?" he said kindly. "What time is Father taking you off?"

"Two o'clock."

"Then I think it might be a good idea if I were to allow you ten minutes or so, and then arrive unexpectedly to pick you up."

"Oh, *thank you!*" said Sally, her eyes like stars.

Then she felt her wig slipping a little and hurriedly adjusted it. The marquess caught the movement and felt a surge of pity. *Poor old girl,* he thought, *having to work for a living at her age and having to wear that awful wig.*

"*Is anyone listening to me? I'm trying to tell you all not to excite Freddie. He's got a dickey heart.*"

Sally was about to confide her strange conversation with Mrs. Stuart to the marquess, but she had been told it all in confidence, and it was all so silly. The marquess would probably laugh at her and tell her that Mrs. Stuart made a habit of plotting her husband's death.

"I'm bored," the Honorable Freddie was telling a dish of currant fritters. "And just look at these." He pushed the fritters pettishly with his fork. "Haven't had those deuced fly cemeteries since I was at school. 'Strordinarily boring house party. The women who are old enough to be interesting just ain't."

His wife cast him such a look of venom that Sally shuddered. Then she reflected bleakly on the tons of etiquette books advising the aspiring classes as to how to behave in society. She wondered if any of them would ever credit the blunt gutter rudeness of some members of the aristocracy. As a schoolgirl, she had been meticulously coached by the Misses Lelongs of Bombay on how to behave and how to eat delicately. And now just look at the duchess picking up three currant fritters at once with her fingers and shoving them into her mouth, and continuing to lay forth on the ball through a spray of crumbs!

But then there was tomorrow to look forward to. If only she could go as Sally Blane and not as Aunt Mabel.

"Now, this is what I call a good brisk day,"

said the duke cheerfully. Sally shivered miserably and longed for some furs.

They were seated in the garden of the Feathers. Great fleecy clouds were flying across the sky, casting their huge shadows over the frosty grass. A starling piped dismally on the lower branch of a bare apple tree. England had been blessed with a long Indian summer, and then the weather had broken all at once, and it just *had* to break on the very day one was stuck in a pub garden with a duke who was in love with the barmaid.

"Here she comes!" whispered the duke, rubbing his hands together.

Out from the inn came a large fat girl carrying a tray and glasses. Sally tried to hide her surprise. *Girl* wasn't exactly the word. For surely Rose was at least in her thirties. She was dressed in a low-cut gown of glaring green and yellow stripes, out of which her enormous bosom threatened to spill. Her face was red and raw and looked as if it had been sandpapered recently. Her large brown eyes were as vacant as a cow's.

"Look at her *arms,*" hissed the duke, wriggling in excitement.

Well, apart from the fact that they were freckled and very powerful-looking, there was not much about them that Sally could see that would possibly explain the duke's infatuation.

"Ah, Rose," sighed the duke. "The last rose of summer."

"Oh, go on, Yur Gryce," said Rose, with a turnip smile. "You do go on. 'E does go on zumthin' orful," she added, nudging Aunt Mabel in the ribs. "This be yur ma?"

"No, my precious," said the duke, leering. "This is Aunt Mabel. Helps gels in distress, don't you know. Finds out all about their love-lives."

Rose put the tray with the two glasses of warm gin—the Duke's plebeian choice—on the table and stared at Sally like a ruminating cow.

"You ain't from *'Ome Chats,* then?" she asked slowly.

Sally nodded.

"Funny," said Rose, balancing the tray on one large hip and staring off into the middle distance. "I wrote to you, mum. Ever such a lovely answer, you give 'un, that you do. 'Marry 'im,' that's what you said. An' that's what I'm going to do."

Sally looked at Rose wildly and then at the

stricken duke. "You don't mean to say . . ." she began.

"Yerse," said Rose dreamily. "I was the pregnant 'ousemaid,' an' I shall marry Jim Finch, 'im that works fer Farmer Andrews. Got a liddle bit o' money put by 'as Jim. Marry 'im, thas what Aunt Mabel said."

The duke cast Sally a look of bewildered hurt. "I didn't know Miss Higgins was a friend of yours when I replied to her letter," said Sally desperately to the duke. "As a matter of fact, I'd never even heard of *you!*" That sounded rather rude, and Sally tried to put it in a gentler way. She laid a comforting hand on the duke's arm, but the duke had already settled on his new role of rejected lover and was prepared to enjoy it to the hilt. But Sally was still too young to know this and watched in alarm as a tear slowly rolled down the duke's cheek.

"Alas! Alas!" he cried to the freezing air.

"What do be the matter, then?" asked Rose, all bucolic concern. She turned to Sally. "Don't 'e like 'is gin, then? Want me to warm it up, mum?"

"No . . . I mean, yes," said Sally, anxious to get rid of Rose. "You must pull yourself together," she told the duke sternly. "What would your tenants say if they could see you like this?"

"The same as they've said all the other times, I suppose," said the Marquess of Seudenham, strolling into the garden and looking heartlessly at his father. "And what on earth are you thinking of, Father, to keep a lady like Aunt Mabel sitting around in this freezing cold? Come, Aunt Mabel."

"But . . ." began Sally helplessly, getting to her feet and looking down at the stricken duke.

"He's enjoying himself," said the marquess, taking her elbow. " 'Bye, Father."

"Go!" cried the duke, striking an attitude, "and leave me to my death!"

"You won't die of a broken heart," said his son callously, "but chances are you'll die of pneumonia if you sit around in this cold much longer." And with that he firmly propelled Sally out of the garden and out of the inn.

Well, Sally had one glorious afternoon, drinking tea in the Pump Room in Bath, gazing into the marquess's blue eyes, and forgetting completely about the lovesick Miss Wyndham who she was supposed to be helping.

He talked lightly and amusingly of plays and

theaters and social gossip, and Sally drank it all in, watching his charming smile and mourning over his gallantry toward this old lady he believed to be in her eighties.

As they were driven back in a well-sprung carriage toward the palace, Sally began to feel a little sad. There must be some way she could manage to meet him without her disguise. But how?

Sally thanked the marquess warmly for her outing and went in search of the library before going to her rooms to change for dinner. She felt sure she would be too excited to sleep much that night, and therefore wanted to find a novel—in English—to pass away the hours.

A thin, colorless man rose to his feet as she entered the library and introduced himself as Mr. Worthing, the ducal secretary.

"And you are Aunt Mabel, of whom I've heard so much," he said with a charming smile, which completely altered his plain features. "I am ready any time to help you with your letters."

"You seem to be very busy," commented Sally, looking at the piles of correspondence on his desk.

110

"I am sending out the invitations to the duchess's ball," he said.

"When is it?" asked Sally.

"On Friday the thirteenth."

"But that's only a week away!"

"Her Grace specializes in impromptu invitations," said Mr. Worthing dryly. "But everyone usually accepts. I have nearly finished. Now, this one is a mistake. Lady Cecily Trevelyn."

"Why a mistake?" asked Sally curiously.

"Because I happen to know that Lady Cecily has left South Africa and will not be arriving in London until two days after the ball."

"Oh." Sally sat down suddenly, her brain working feverishly.

"Is Lady Cecily a debutante?" asked Sally suddenly. "And who is she?"

"Lady Cecily is the ward of the Earl and Countess of Hammering, who were visiting their estates in South Africa. Lady Cecily's parents, the Duke and Duchess of Dervere, died when she was a baby."

"How sad," said Sally. "Is she my age?"

Mr. Worthing looked in surprise at the agitated old lady.

"You cannot mean Lady Cecily, since she is

nineteen years old," he said delicately. "I assume you are referring to Lady Hammering, who is about . . . er . . . forty."

"Much younger than I," said Sally, recovering from her blunder.

Her brain seemed to be working at an enormous rate. "I have it!" said Sally with a bland smile. "I remember hearing that the Earl and Countess of Hammering have, in fact, arrived in London. Yesterday, I believe."

"Really!" said Mr. Worthing. "I am usually very well informed of the comings and goings of the duchess's friends, but I take your word for it, of course."

"In fact," rushed on Sally, "they are by way of being personal friends of mine, and I have to travel to London . . . er . . . tomorrow, and I could take the invitation with me."

"Well," he said slowly, "that would be very kind of you."

A dismal thought suddenly struck Sally.

"I suppose," she said, looking down and twisting at a loose thread on her mittens, "that the duke and duchess are very well acquainted with Lady Cecily. Known her since childhood."

"Oh, no," said Mr. Worthing. "As far as I

know they've never set eyes on her. She's not come out yet, so to speak, so no one's really seen her."

Sally breathed an inward sigh of relief. Lady Cecily would go to the ball, represented by Sally Blane!

Sally thanked Mr. Worthing effusively for the invitation, whereupon he replied with mild surprise that the thanks were all on his side. She made her escape and went in search of the duchess, to explain that it was imperative that Aunt Mabel return to London to see her doctor, that Aunt Mabel would unfortunately not be attending the ball, but that Aunt Mabel would definitely return on the day after in case further counseling was needed.

CHAPTER FIVE

"I can't possibly do it!" protested Miss Fleming, raising her hands in horror.

"You've got to," said Sally grimly. "I must have a chaperon."

Both women were sitting in the living room of their Bloomsbury flat, and Miss Frimp was visiting a cousin. On the table between them lay the invitation to the Earl and Countess of Harrington and their ward, Lady Cecily.

"We'll be found out," moaned Miss Fleming. "I mean, we're expected to stay there a day before the ball. Ample time for anyone to discover we're impostors. *Think*, Sally. If someone wrote asking you for your advice in this matter, you would tell them very sternly to forget about the whole thing."

"I'm in love with him," said Sally flatly, as if this admission answered all protests.

"Aren't you just in love with the title?" pleaded Miss Fleming. "Then there's my job to consider. What will I tell Mr. Wingles?"

"You forget," pointed out Sally ruthlessly, "that you told me Mr. Wingles was going on holiday next week and that you planned to take a few days off."

"But—"

"No one will find out," said Sally earnestly. "No one."

"What has Mr. Barton to say about all this?"

"Nothing," said Sally blithely, "because I didn't tell him. He doesn't care where I work, so long as I work."

"But the cost—"

"I have money saved," said Sally. "Enough to pay for two simply ripping ball gowns. Just think! A real live ducal ball!"

Miss Matilda Fleming looked wonderingly at her young friend. Sally looked as pretty and elf-like as she had done on that hot day when she had arrived in Fleet Street. She was, however, Miss Fleming reflected, as tough as old boots under that misleading exterior. Miss Fleming had always prided herself on being a tough businesswoman, but little Sally, she thought with surprise, was by far the stronger personality.

But she took one last stand. "I won't do it," she said grimly. "Just wait till Jessie Frimp hears of this!"

But later on, to Miss Fleming's dismay, Miss Frimp thought there was no harm in the impersonation of Lady Cecily, not knowing that Miss Frimp was frightened that if Miss Fleming did not go then she, Miss Frimp, would be nagged into it by Sally, already having a better assessment of the force of Sally's personality than Miss Fleming.

"It's not a crime, after all," said Miss Frimp.

"I thought impersonating a peer of the realm was a crime," said Miss Fleming.

"Well, you'll only be going as a sort of *companion*," urged Miss Frimp. "Anyway, it says peer of the realm, not peeress."

"Same thing," said Miss Fleming gloomily.

"And what if they do find out?" demanded Sally, striding up and down the room and waving her arms in her excitement. "The whole focus will be on me, not you. I tell you what, Matilda. I'll accept the invitation, say my guardians, the earl and countess, are indisposed, but that I shall be arriving with my chaperon, Miss Matilda Fleming. There! That way you won't be impersonating anyone. And . . . and . . . I could always say you didn't know I wasn't Lady Cecily."

"It's no use," said Matilda. "I just can't do it."

The Bath train rattled through the bleak November landscape. "I just can't do it," Miss Fleming was still saying. "My dear, did you *see* some of the other guests on this train? The clothes, the maids, the footmen."

"We look very grand," said Sally stoutly, although privately her heart misgave her. Her savings had not been nearly enough to equip them with an adequate wardrobe, although Miss Fleming had insisted on paying for her own ball gown.

Sally had had to buy most of the other clothes secondhand, and their luggage smelled suspiciously of gasoline and stale bread crumbs—the gasoline to clean the wool frocks, and the stale bread crumbs to clean Sally's white silk ball gown.

Sally's only jewelry was a small dog collar of pearls. No one wore diamonds in the country, she told herself firmly. All the etiquette books said so. But she was sure, somehow, that the rest of the guests did not read etiquette books, or if they did, they paid them not the slightest heed.

How fast the train seemed to be going. How it bore them inexorably nearer to their destination.

Smoke billowed out over the ridges of the plowed fields, and flocks of rooks wheeled against the lowering sky.

Sally tried to remember the handsome marquess, and found she could not. Her whole stay at the palace seemed to have been some extraordinary dream. She had told Miss Fleming about Mrs. Stuart threatening to kill her husband and the duke's infatuation for the barmaid, and Miss Fleming had said forthrightly that they all sounded mad and that there was probably inbreeding somewhere in the duke's family.

Carriages were waiting to convey the guests to the palace. Only a few, of which Lady Cecily was one, had been honored with an invitation to stay before and after the ball. Sally had accepted the invitation, saying that the earl and countess were indisposed, but that her companion, Miss Matilda Fleming, would be accompanying her.

But Sally did not grasp quite how ridiculous, quite how hopeless, her situation was until she saw her traveling companions. For sharing the carriage to the palace with Sally and Miss Fleming were the Guthrie sisters. The Guthrie sisters were not of good family, in fact, their father had begun his career with a small bicycle shop in Cambridge. But he had opened his shop right at the beginning of the heyday of that machine, and his business had grown and prospered until he became very wealthy indeed. To add to his dizzy success, he had launched on society his two beautiful daughters, Daisy and Dolly.

Although it was still considered "unfortunate" to be blond, no one could find any fault with the Guthrie sisters. Their beauty was of the blond, porcelain type. They had delicate little noses and delicate arched brows over large, well-shaped blue eyes. Their busts were large and their waists tiny, and it was whispered that their exquisite hourglass figures were all their own, neither of them having to resort to horsehair pads to achieve the fashionable silhouette.

But their crowning beauty was that both were

quite brainless, and in a society that viewed intelligence with distrust, this was the final seal of acceptability. The jealous might mutter over the Guthrie sisters' plebeian origins, but for the most part society adored them both.

Stupid they might have been in the worlds of books, music, art, and politics, but in the worlds of romance, husbands, and ballrooms, they had native animal cunning. They were natural hunters and had learned at an early age how to kill with a flashing glance, how to wound with a haughty turn of the head, and how to raise wild hopes with a small sigh.

Daisy and Dolly did not have much time for other women, unless they were the sisters or mothers of eligible men, and so they prattled on as if Sally and Miss Fleming were invisible. Sally wondered why two such diamonds of the first water had managed to come through one Season unwed, but it soon transpired that both sisters hoped to marry the marquess, and both were confident of success.

Although there was a year between their ages, they looked remarkably alike, except that Daisy's hair was somewhat darker.

I am cursed with blondes, thought Sally

gloomily. *I was mad to come. Even poor Miss Wyndham won't stand a chance with this precious pair around.*

Dolly and Daisy, unlike Miss Wyndham, were blessed with pussycat naughtiness. Certainly their girlish wriggles, shrieks, and giggles annoyed Sally immensely, but she was clever enough to realize that most gentlemen would interpret it all as innocent charm.

"We have an ally on our side," Dolly was saying. "The duchess told Lady Brainwater, and *she* told Mama, that the duchess wants Paul—*duveen name*—to settle for one of us."

Daisy wrinkled her pretty brow. "But he's got ever such a reputation, Doll'. He was keeping that opera singer for ever so long."

Dolly shrugged. "Better they have mistresses before they're married than after."

Miss Fleming shot the girls a repressive glance, and the Guthrie sisters stared back at her impertinently and then collapsed into girlish giggles.

Sally was glad when they arrived, for she had decided what to do.

She would hide behind the other guests, send Miss Fleming with a message to the duchess, to

121

say that Lady Cecily was indisposed and had to return immediately to town—and escape.

Her clothes felt shabbier and dowdier and more secondhand by the minute. Now, Sally was a very pretty girl, but even the prettiest women need someone around to tell them so. Emily had always been considered the beauty of the family, and when Sally had taken her hair out of braids and made her transformation from ugly duckling into swan, there was no fond mother to tell her so. She had become so accustomed to the role of Aunt Mabel that sometimes her mind played tricks on her, and she felt as if she really were a little old lady with specs and wrinkles.

As they shuffled into line behind the other guests who were being greeted by the duke and duchess in the main hall, Sally muttered her plan of escape to Miss Fleming, and that austere lady looked noticeably relieved.

But the duke and duchess were joined suddenly by the marquess just as the Guthrie sisters were tripping forward, little rosebud mouths uttering birdlike cries of welcome, eyes flashing killing glances in the direction of the marquess.

Sally's heart did several somersaults, and she gazed in open adoration at the marquess until

Miss Fleming brought her to her senses by jabbing a bony elbow in her ribs.

Wonder of wonders! The Guthrie sisters were fluttering and charming for all they were worth, and a faint shadow of boredom crossed the marquess's handsome face.

Gone was Sally's thought of escape. Hope burst forth anew.

When it was Sally's turn she introduced herself as Lady Cecily Trevelyn, apologized for the absence of her guardians, and presented with pretty grace Miss Fleming. Miss Fleming noticed sourly that the marquess had taken Sally's little hand in his and showed no sign of releasing it. Miss Fleming thought Sally a very pretty girl indeed, but she had never told her so, considering that it was rather vulgar to make personal comments to one's friends.

"Do you ride, Lady Cecily?" the marquess was asking.

"Of course," lied Sally. Unusual in a girl of her age and Indian background, but Sally had never learned to ride. The Misses Lelongs had frowned on riding lessons, considering that horses did quite terrible things to the hymen, sidesaddle or not. Not that they would have dreamed of voicing such a coarse idea, for they contented themselves with conveying the dangers by solemn shakes of the head.

So Sally had never ridden. But she was not going to say so, for she was sure it was all terribly easy. All one did was sit on the beast and let it carry one along.

"I thought of going for a canter before tea, Lady Cecily," said the marquess. "Around four o'clock. Perhaps you might like to join me? I can show you something of the estate."

"I would love to," said Sally fervently.

His face became a well-bred blank, and Sally cursed inwardly. She had been too eager.

"I don't have a riding habit," said Sally truthfully—and untruthfully. "My maid forgot to pack it."

"Mother will find you something," said the marquess.

"Yes, indeed," said the duchess, coming forward. "But, Paul, is the whole party going out riding, or just you and Lady Cecily?"

Now, the marquess had just been regretting asking Sally, since she seemed overly eager, and had been about to extend his invitation to several of the others. Since his mother showed every sign of putting a spoke in his wheel, he decided that Lady Cecily was as charming as he had initially thought and wished again to see her on her own.

"No, just Lady Cecily," he said. "You have invited so many attractive young women, Mother, that you can't expect me to entertain them all at once."

The duchess looked as if she were about to protest, but fortunately more guests arrived, and Sally promised to meet the marquess at the stables at four and made her escape with Miss Fleming.

The rooms allocated to them were not so grand as the ones given to Aunt Mabel, but they were prettily furnished for all that. Miss Fleming stood looking grimly at their trunks. "I shall tell the maid not to unpack," she said.

"But we're staying *now*," said Sally. "Don't you see how easily they accepted me? And in two hours time I'll be going riding with Paul."

"With . . . oh, the Marquess of Seudenham. And *then* we leave," said Miss Fleming hopefully.

Sally avoided her gaze. "We'll see," she mumbled. "Wasn't it marvelous the way he looked so bored with the gushings of the Guthrie sisters?"

"Sophisticated young men about town often *look* bored with that sort of nonsense," commented Miss Fleming, "but they marry them just the same. Makes them feel superior. Little woman, and all that. Besides, the Guthrie girls have considerable dowries."

"The marquess is very rich. He doesn't need to marry for money," pointed out Sally, sitting down by the fire.

"My dear child," said Miss Fleming acidly, beginning to remove her hatpins. "Whenever did an English aristocrat sneer at money? The marquess has considerable estates of his own, and they must cost a mint to keep up."

"I thought he lived here," said Sally naively.

Miss Fleming gave a superior titter. "Oh, no. The marquess lives at Seudenham Manor in Surrey. It's almost as big as this place."

Sally looked at her friend, round-eyed. It seemed . . . well . . . *indecent* to have parents who owned all this, and yet to have nearly as much yourself.

Miss Fleming, having divested herself of her beaver hat, announced she was going to lie down until five o'clock tea. Miss Fleming was accustomed to country house visits. When the owner of the *Daily Bugle* summoned the editor, Mr. Wingles, to a house party, Mr. Wingles always took Miss Fleming along by way of protection.

The great palace seemed much livelier than before, with the voices of the other guests rising and falling from the nearby rooms.

Sally looked out of the window. They were at the top of the house, on the fourth floor, under the attics in the west wing. Over to the left she could see the clock tower over the stables, and up above the clock tower loomed a darkening sky.

Oh, please don't let it rain, prayed Sally, *or I won't have a chance!*

Two hours seemed a long time to wait. But a maid arrived with a smart black gaberdine and velvet riding habit over one arm and a smart black riding topper to go with it—". . . compliments of Her Grace."

The outfit looked brand new, and Sally was to find out later that it belonged to Miss Wyndham, who went riding as little as possible.

She spent most of the two hours trying it on and pacing mannishly up and down the room, feeling like a heroine in a novel. She weaved all sorts of fantasies around the forthcoming ride. In some, she would be thrown from her horse, and the marquis would clasp her in his arms and say he loved her. In others, *he* would be thrown from his horse, and *she* would clasp him in her arms and cradle his poor bloodied head on her lap, and then spend endless gorgeous days nursing him back to health.

At precisely ten minutes to four Sally left the palace by a side entrance and made her way by a sort of circular road that led to the stables.

The marquess was already there, talking to the head groom. He gave her a somewhat indifferent nod by way of a greeting, and Sally's heart fell. The marquess was, in fact, wondering what had come over him to single out Lady Cecily for this honor. He had learned that his mother had put it about that he was looking for a wife, and he was beginning to feel hunted. The duchess had invited quite a bevy of beauties, and everywhere he went in the palace, glowing eyes stared at him from rooms and corridors.

While he continued to chat with the groom, Sally eyed the tall, nasty looking horse the groom was holding and wondered how she could mount something like that in what she was wearing. The riding habit had been made by John Barker of Kensington for 105 shillings a top price. The dress itself had a very tightly cut bodice, lightly boned to the waist, and the skirt was cut to accommodate the right knee when mounting sidesaddle.

Over the bodice went a very tightly cut waistcoat. Now, most ladies "buttoned up" after they were mounted, but, of course, no one had told Sally that, and she was already having difficulty breathing.

At last the marquess turned his gaze on her. Sally preened a little. She knew that for once she was wearing something that became her.

"Sanders," said the marquess, leading the groom forward, "we need a mount for Lady Cecily."

"I've put the sidesaddle on Thunderbird," said Sanders.

"Is that Thunderbird?" asked Sally faintly, looking up at the black snorting animal.

"Yes, my lady," said Sanders. "Quiet as a lamb."

Sally bit her lip. "H-haven't y-you anything *smaller*?"

The marquess had fortunately gone off to attend to his own mount. A faint look of scorn flickered across Sanders's mahogany face. "Well, I dunno, my lady. Reckon there's that slug, Dandelion."

"Dandelion will do perfectly, Sanders," said Sally in what she hoped was a very autocratic manner.

Sanders gave a faint shrug and led Thunderbird away toward the stables.

Dandelion, when at last saddled up, proved to be what Sally hoped he would be from his nursery name. He was a broad-backed piebald horse with an expression of patient suffering.

"As long as you're happy, my lady," said Sanders as Sally walked to the mounting block. "Dandelion's an old broken-down show jumper and a bit sluggish."

Meanwhile the marquess had swung himself easily into the saddle of an enormous hunter. Sally, more by good luck than anything else, succeeded in getting herself into the sidesaddle on Dandelion's back without much mishap, apart from the fact that her waistcoat buttons snapped under the strain and shot off all around the stable yard like bullets.

Master and groom averted their eyes and politely refrained from comment.

Sally and the marquess ambled out of the stable yard, and all Sally's fears left her. There was nothing to this horse riding after all. She relaxed her feverish grip on the reins and looked about her with pleasure. She had recovered quickly from the embarrassment of the popping buttons.

The marquess was a little in the lead. "We'll take the bridle path along the other side of the lake," he called over his shoulder, and Sally called back a cheery "Right-ho!" feeling no end of a horsewoman.

Everything went very well as they moved slowly along the cinnamon-colored path beside the ruffled black waters of the lake. "That very pretty rotunda over there," called the marquess, pointing to a marble colonnaded building situated on a knoll, "was built by the second duke."

Sally was about to make some reply, but Dandelion had decided to amble sideways along the path and was beginning to take up all her attention.

Then the marquess began to move his horse into a canter. Sally looked after his disappearing figure in dismay. So did Dandelion. At last

Dandelion judged correctly that the limp weight on his back was devoid of mastery and decided to take the law into his hooves. He tossed his head and set off at a canter along the path after the marquess.

It was then that Sally realized there was more to riding than she could have possibly imagined.

Up and down went Dandelion, and up and down went Sally, like a sack of potatoes, slipping and sliding and always just nearly falling off, and always just managing to haul herself back with the pommel.

The marquess left the lake and cantered along a long, narrow stretch of beaten track that led up a gentle slope towards Sally thought bleakly, infinity.

And then the marquess urged his horse into a gallop.

For one split second Browning's lines ran madly through Sally's head: "I galloped, Dirck galloped, we galloped all three," for she knew as sure as she knew anything that Dandelion was going to follow suit. And sure enough off he went like an arrow from a bow.

Now, apart from the fact that one gets hurtled along at a frightening pace, a galloping horse does not chuck one about the place as much as a cantering horse, and so with Sally hanging onto the pommel, Dandelion streamed off in pursuit, up the hill and down the other side. Sleet was beginning to fall and stung her face. There is nothing like novice horse riding for working up a good religious fervor, and Sally certainly prayed as she had never prayed before. At the bottom of the hill, the path swerved sharply to the left at the front of a five-barred gate.

Sally left off praying and opened her mouth to call "Whoa," but, alas, in her extreme fright, she called out "Hup!" instead and Dandelion, hearing that command from his old show jumping days and being full of oats, went straight for that five-barred gate.

The marquess, hearing the frantic thud of hooves over the sound of his own horse, had reined in and turned just in time to see a splendid sight.

Dandelion sailed over the gate with an inch to spare, with Sally clinging for dear life to his back. Some age-old instinct told her at the last minute to lift her bottom out of the saddle before Dandelion landed. He then galloped hell-for-leather twice around the field and then slowed and stopped finally, putting his head down and amiably beginning to crop the grass.

Stunned and shaken, Sally moved her grip automatically from the pommel to the reins and sat as still as a stone.

"By Jove!" called the marquess, dismounting and opening the gate. "What splendid horsemanship. I didn't know old Dandelion still had it in him! Wonderful riding!"

He stood smiling up at her, and Sally smiled back, a blinding smile, a wonderful smile. And the marquess was enchanted. He did not know that it was the smile of a girl who could not believe she was still alive.

"Come along!" cried the marquess, all boyish enthusiasm. "I'll race you back."

And in one split second love nearly changed to hate in Sally's bosom.

"I think poor old Dandelion has had enough, and one must always consider one's horse," she said sanctimoniously. "Let's just amble and—and—talk."

"Right-ho!" he said gaily. He held open the gate for her, and, fortunately for Sally, Dandelion *was* tired and realized it was nearly feeding time, and so he ambled placidly out of the gate. The marquess mounted and this time rode beside Sally.

"I think that was the most gallant jump I have ever seen," he said, enthused, and Sally privately agreed with him.

"You hunt, of course. There's a meet after the ball."

I can't, thought Sally wildly. *I just can't.* Aloud she said, "I have hunted, yes, but not the fox. I have been out of England a great deal. Pigsticking, you know."

The marquess surveyed her in amazement. "Pigsticking! In Africa?"

Too late, Sally realized her mistake. "Well, it was not precisely Africa. We were in India— Bombay, for a time."

"I've never heard of a woman going pigsticking in *any* country," said the marquess suspiciously. "Tell me about it."

And Sally did, for Sally could. Hadn't she listened to boring after boring story about that brutal sport at dinner party after dinner party?

So she discoursed at length about the typical pigsticking meets, which would start long before dawn because it was too hot to ride in the heat of the day; of the long line of riders moving across country, usually in heats of three, a few lengths ahead of the beat; of the pandemonium that would break out when a boar was sighted, every beater yelling *"Woh jata!"* or "There he goes!" and the nearest heat galloping off in arrow formation with the man in front shouting, "On! On! On!"; of the incredible speeds of the horses, usually Australian walers—from New South Wales—that seemed to be able to float across the country.

Sally went on to explain how to deliver the spear correctly over the boar's shoulder and into his shoulder blade. And the marquess listened, entranced. Although he had heard most of it before, he thought it marvelous and amazing that this elflike creature should be capable of such bravery and experience. He was so engrossed in her lecture that he kept his horse to a safe amble and was barely aware, until they were once more moving along beside the lake, that the sleet had changed to large flakes of snow that were gradually blotting out the landscape.

He thought Sally's indifference to the weather was typical of the girl, not knowing that Sally was freezing to death but would have endured anything other than another gallop, and was trying to keep his attention away from horse riding by going on about pigsticking until she felt she was beginning to bore herself.

When they finally arrived at the stables, Sally was making a great effort to control the shaking of her knees. She felt battered and bruised all over.

The marquess held up his arms to lift her down, and she fell heavily against him. But not for worlds would she let him know what a physical wreck she felt, and so she smiled up into his eyes with a flirtatious twinkle in her own so that he would think she had collapsed deliberately against him.

After a slight look of surprise the marquess held her very close and then released her, turning away to shout something to the head groom, Sanders, and therefore sparing himself the sight of his fair partner reeling like a drunk as her weak and trembling legs fought for balance.

By the time he had turned back, she had recovered enough to walk with him to the palace without staggering or falling. Much as she loved him, all Sally longed for was a hot bath. But . . .

"Good Heavens! Teatime already," said the marquess, pulling out his half hunter and staring at it. "Don't bother to change. We are not very muddy. Only rather wet."

Sally groaned inwardly. As he led her through the hall she caught a glimpse of herself in a long looking glass and almost started in surprise. Apart from the missing buttons on her waistcoat, she saw in amazement that she looked possibly more elegant and assured than she had ever done in her life. The black topper was remarkably becoming, and, underneath it, not even a strand of hair had come loose from its moorings.

Quite a surprising number of people were assembled in the large drawing room, drinking tea. The Guthrie sisters descended on the marquess with little chirping cries and bore him off, one on either side. He cast an anguished look of mock despair over his shoulder at Sally, which every lady in the room noted, hating Sally accordingly.

With relief Sally saw the trim and upright figure of Miss Fleming and headed in that lady's direction.

"I'm dying," she muttered as Miss Fleming handed her a cup of tea. "I'd never ridden a horse before, and never, ever will I ride one again."

"I say, Lady Cecily," said a voice at her elbow, "allow me to introduce myself. My name's Firkin, Peter Firkin. Just heard Paul telling evcrybody about your marvelous jump. Jolly good, haw. You'll show us all at the meet on Saturday."

"I don't think—" began Sally weakly.

"Everyone's turning out to see you go through your paces, don't you know. You must tell me all about the time you went pigsticking."

"You *what*?" interposed Miss Fleming.

Sally suddenly put down her teacup with a hand that shook. "Later, Mr. Firkin," she said. "Miss Fleming, please come upstairs with me. I do not like to stand around in all my dirt."

Miss Fleming cast a longing look toward a plate of cucumber sandwiches and decided to make the best of it. She collared a footman and asked that their afternoon tea be served to them in their rooms and bore Sally off.

Sally managed bravely until the door of her room closed behind her. Then she threw herself on the bed and burst into tears.

"He didn't . . . he *couldn't have*," exclaimed

Miss Fleming, who always believed that men were only after one thing.

"No! No!" wailed Sally. "I hurt all over, and I was so frightened, and now I am to go hunting."

Miss Fleming sat on the edge of the bed and took Sally's limp hand in her own.

"Look here, Sally," she said. "Have you paused to think what on earth you can possibly *do* even if the Marquess falls head over heels in love with you? By the ball tomorrow night, he will only have known Lady Cecily a short time. A man like that does not propose on such short notice. And what if he does? You will then need to tell him that you are not Lady Cecily Trevelyn, a duke's daughter, but plain Sally Blane of Bloomsbury, who works as Aunt Mabel."

"Oh, don't!" wailed Sally. "I know it's all been such a mistake. I fantasized that he would forgive me when I told him . . . but now I've already deceived him further by pretending I can ride."

"Then let us make our excuses and leave," said Miss Fleming briskly. "If we hurry, perhaps we can catch the seven o'clock train from Bath."

Sally sat up and dried her tears, looking mulish. "And leave him in the clutches of those Guthrie girls? Never! I've gone through all this to go to this ball, and go I jolly well will!"

"And on the stroke of midnight you'll have to turn back into Aunt Mabel," pointed out Miss Fleming.

"Oh, I don't need to turn into Aunt Mabel until after the hunt," pointed out Sally, looking considerably more cheerful.

"You can't possibly go on that hunt. You can't even ride. You don't know the first thing about it."

"I can read a book on the subject," said Sally, all mad reason.

"It's a pity you can't marry the man," said Miss Fleming acidly. "You would fit in very well here. They're all mad. That Mrs. Stuart was telling everyone before you arrived that 'poor old Freddie' was due to pop off any minute, and the man just stood there looking like a silly sheep. And for your information, Miss Wyndham is not in love with your Paul. The poor girl is head over heels in love with that ass, Peter Firkin."

Sally opened her mouth in surprise, but at that moment two footmen arrived, bearing their tea.

"Oh, splendid!" cried Miss Fleming. "Hot muffins and strawberry jam. Come along, Sally. There is nothing like a muffin and a good cup of tea to restore anyone to sanity."

But Sally could barely wait until the servants had left before she burst out with, "But *how* can Miss Wyndham be in love with Peter Firkin when Paul is around?"

"No accounting for taste," said Miss Fleming, her mouth full of muffin.

"I had better go and tell her," said Sally, decidedly. "I thought she was talking about Paul. And Peter Firkin is in love with *her,* for he told me so."

"You'll need to wait until you're Aunt Mabel again," pointed out her friend.

Sally sighed and resigned herself to tea. She thought over her behavior of the afternoon and decided after much hard thought that she had been too bold, too independent. Everyone knew —for hadn't Aunt Mabel counseled her readers so?—that gentlemen liked soft, feminine, helpless women. She should not have put up such a brave front. She should have told him she felt weak and shaky. She must change her strategy.

She still felt sore all over. She would tell him prettily that very fact this evening.

And she had every opportunity to do so. For Lady Cecily had been given that much-coveted place next to the marquess at the dinner table.

The Guthrie sisters tittered behind their fans and wondered what Paul could see in such an insignificant creature. The duchess looked at Sally speculatively and rather liked what she saw. Sally was looking her very best, courtesy of the Annual Sale on Behalf of the Society for Indigent Gentlewomen. She was wearing a blond lace blouse that had a pretty neckline. Her masses of fine hair had been prettily dressed over her forehead in the very latest fashion by Miss Fleming, who showed unexpected expertise with the curling iron. The dog collar of pearls clasped around her neck emphasized the creaminess of her skin. Her new pink corset created that necessary effect of the monobosom, since it was downright indecent to betray the fact that a woman possessed two breasts.

Sally was prepared for the awful food and had the advantage in that respect of the other guests. She had eaten a great deal of cakes and sandwiches at tea, remembering that tea was excellent, while dinner was foul. She was therefore at leisure to pick at her food and start her campaign of persuading the marquess that she was a frail and helpless female.

Sally prettily, and with many deprecatory giggles, complained of her aches and pains and received nothing more than a blank look of disinterest from the marquess, who, after listening politely to her complaints, nodded in a rather bored way and then turned his attention to a ravishing redhead on his left, leaving Sally to the dull conversation of Sir Sydney Chelmsford, on *her* other side.

Sally bit her lip, wondering what she had done wrong. Now, Sally had acquired quite a fund of wisdom through her job as Aunt Mabel, but it was all in the abstract, so to speak, and there was nothing quite like firsthand experience. She was too young to have realized the sad fact that the most attractive and charming men were unfortunately the kind who, after the first fine, careless rapture was over, were the very ones to go into a sulk if one was sick, crashing the breakfast tray on one's knees with a contemptuous look. But God help one if *they* were ill themselves. A slight cold would be interpreted as influenza, and acute indigestion as cancer. And unless one was resigned to that hard fact and stopped being weak and clinging and expecting the strong man to give one sympathy, then the man would be apt to up and off with some female with a face like a boot and a soul like whipcord.

But Sally did realize that the marquess had smiled on her when she was being bold and brave, and so she lent an ear to his conversation with the dashing redhead, seeking for an opportunity to recapture his attention.

When he at last turned to her again Sally said brightly, "Tell me, do you think a modern woman should have a career?"

"Indeed, yes," said the marquess, showing interest again. "I think every woman should have some sort of job before she is married."

"What do you do for a living?" asked Sally in a mocking voice.

He looked at her in surprise. "Why, the same as your brothers," he said. "How is John, by the way?"

Sally gulped. "Very well. I have not had an opportunity to speak to him since my return."

"Hardly surprising," said the marquess, "since he is in the West Indies."

"Yes," said Sally, deciding not to elaborate any further.

"You know," went on the marquess, "it's those eyes of yours. They remind me of something."

"What?" breathed Sally, agog for a compliment.

He studied her for some moments. "Aunt Mabel," he said.

Sally hurriedly lowered her eyes to her plate.

"Yes," he went on. "Now, there's a career woman for you."

"Who on earth is Aunt Mabel?" asked Sally, following the question with what she hoped would be a rippling laugh, but it came out more as a croak.

"You *have* been out of touch," he mocked. "Aunt Mabel is the lady from *Home Chats* who answers all our problems."

"Oh, I don't understand how people can demean themselves by writing to a complete stranger for advice," said Sally, anxious to disassociate herself from Aunt Mabel.

"You surprise me. I would have thought you had more understanding," he said lightly. "There are an awful lot of people who would

146

rather ask a complete stranger for advice than their immediate family. And don't let my mother hear you say so. She invited Aunt Mabel down here to ask her advice."

"What about?"

"About me. Mother thought I was going to marry Miss Wyndham, and she thought the young lady was too good for me."

"Quite right," said Sally, and then realized her mistake, as he raised his eyebrows in surprise.

"I mean," she rushed on, anxious to cover her gaffe, "I am sure your mother knew what was best for you."

"I am not a child, Lady Cecily," he said, and turned his attention back to the redhead.

Blast! thought Sally. But then she remembered the duchess saying that the marquess liked his women to have a bit of vice in them. She must be bolder.

To her extreme irritation Sir Sydney Chelmsford turned out to have heard of her pigsticking exploits and was prepared to cap them with several very long and boring stories of his own.

Sally could only be relieved when the duchess

rose to her feet, indicating that the ladies should leave the gentlemen to their port.

In the drawing room, Sally was extremely alarmed when Miss Fleming pointed out that it was a miracle that none of these ladies turned out to have known the real Lady Cecily. This was a snag that Sally had not even considered, and so she lurked in Miss Fleming's grim shadow, expecting at any moment to be exposed.

Apart from the Misses Guthrie, there were a number of good-looking girls with their hopeful mamas, and the Duchess was surrounded by quite a court of females trying to ingratiate themselves with Her Grace.

All the ladies were dressed in their best, and very few had learned that diamonds were considered vulgar in the country. Sally felt her dog collar of pearls, which had looked so handsome in the privacy of her bedroom, pale into insignificance beside the blaze of diamonds and rubies and emeralds and sapphires.

At last they were joined by the gentlemen, and it transpired they were going to play charades.

By some sort of unspoken agreement, the ladies had decided to exclude Sally from the festivities, and Sally was too frightened of exposure to put herself forward. Therefore she had the doubtful pleasure of watching the marquess playing Romeo to Dolly Guthrie's Juliet and thought sourly that these silly, childish games would go on forever. But at last the charades were over, and the guests were urged to give an impromptu concert. Again the Guthrie girls were to the fore, singing selections from Gilbert and Sullivan with weak, little voices and amazing aplomb.

The evening was saved for Sally by the Honorable Freddie. Screwing his monocle in his eye, he announced, despite groans of protest, that he was going to recite.

Undeterred by his wife's loud and acid comments, he rose to his feet, cleared his throat, and declared, "I am going to recite one of the finest and most moving bits of poetry I've ever read. It's by a Scotch scribe-chappie called William McGonagall, entitled, "The Tay Bridge Disaster.""

"He's got to go. He's really got to go," observed Mrs. Stuart to the world at large, but with the exception of Sally, they thought his wife meant he had simply to leave the room, whereas

Sally alone knew that Mrs. Stuart meant leave the planet.

The guests politely listened to the first verse in amazement and then began to talk loudly and rudely among themselves. William McGonagall was, after all, an acquired taste. That Victorian poet never troubled his head with meter or form. As long as each line of verse rhymed somehow with the one before it, he was perfectly happy and expected his readers to feel the same way.

Only Sally and the marquess moved slightly forward to listen in awe to the Honorable Freddie's rendering.

By the time they converged at the end of the room near the fireplace, which served as the "stage," Freddie was declaiming the third verse.

"But when the train came near to Wormit
      Bay,
Boreas he did loud and angry bray,
And shook the central girders of the Bridge
      of Tay
On the last Sabbath day of 1879,
Which will be remembered for a very long
      time."

* * *

Sally suddenly felt the marquess's eye upon her and was overcome by a desire to giggle. Behind them in the room, the guests chattered on regardless. In front of them, Freddie was giving the "Tay Bridge Disaster" his heart and soul.

At last he reached the final stanza.

"It must have been an awful sight,
To witness in the dusky moonlight,
While the Storm Fiend did laugh, and angry did bray,
Along the Railway Bridge of the Silv'ry Tay,
Oh! ill-fated Bridge of the Silv'ry Tay,
I must now conclude my lay
By telling the world fearlessly and without the least dismay,
That your central girders would not have given way,
At least many sensible men do say,
Had they been supported on each side with buttresses,
At least many sensible men confesses,
For the stronger we our houses do build,
The less chance we have of being killed."

* * *

"Remove me from here," muttered Sally to the marquess in a stifled voice, her face buried in her handkerchief.

He nodded and piloted her out deftly through the guests and into the great, shadowy hall. "Lady Cecily," he said severely, "you are incorrigible."

"I can't help it," wailed Sally, laughing till the tears ran down her face. "It was so awfully funny, and there was Mrs. Stuart plotting like mad to poison her husband."

"Oh, nonsense!" said the marquess. "She may look like that sometimes, but Mrs. Stuart is very fond of Freddie—in her fashion. Oh, do stop laughing, or you'll start me off. Come here, and I'll dry your eyes."

He pulled her gently toward him, and Sally stopped laughing and stared up at him, wide-eyed. The hall was suddenly very quiet as he looked down at her in dawning surprise, dawning awareness, a clean handkerchief forgotten in his hand.

The great hall was only lit by two oil lamps. Outside, the snow whispered against the windows. A voice, louder than the rest, in the drawing room sounded out very near the door.

He is going to kiss me, thought Sally wildly. *He only likes girls with a bit of vice in them. I must encourage him. . . .*

Closing her eyes, and summoning up all her reserves of courage, she put her arms around his neck.

The blue eyes above hers gleamed with a wicked light, and she closed her own. His lips descended on hers, at first surprisingly warm and boyish and innocent.

Then the very adult emotions behind his lips took over, and in one moment Sally lost her emotional virginity. She had often thought of some man who would hold hands with her and kiss her and then—naturally—marry her; some sort of cosy extension of a school friend. But never had she imagined anything like this sinking, burning, melting feeling. She never wanted to let go. She wanted it to go on forever and ever, his lips burning against her own while the clocks in the hall ticked busily in the background, the enormous log fire crackled on the hearth, and the snow whispered urgently against the windowpanes.

"Oh, I can't bear it! I just can't bear it! It should be me. Me and Rose. Oh, Rose."

"Damn and double bloody *damn!*" said the marquess, releasing Sally so abruptly that she nearly fell, and swinging around.

Unnoticed by both of them, the duke had been slumped in a high wing chair in the shadows, a little bit away from the fire.

"Oh, go to bed, Father," snapped the marquess, exasperated.

"It's all right for you," mumbled the duke sulkily. "Kissing and canoodling with all and sundry."

Poor Sally. One bare moment ago she had felt as if all the love songs and all the romance in the world had been centered in her small body. And now it all withered and died before that "canoodling with all and sundry."

She gave the marquess a shaky little good night and fled up the stairs, only realizing when she was in the safety of her room that she had left the field clear open to the other ladies. Oh, dear! What did he think of her? Did he think her fast? Did he think of her at all?

The evening was made worse by the arrival of Miss Fleming, who reported that the party was now playing children's games, and that in blindman's buff, the marquess had seized Dolly Guthrie around the waist. Furthermore she, Miss Fleming, wondered what the youth of today was coming to.

If he gives me a cold look tomorrow, thought Sally desperately, *then I shall leave.*

But the next day, the marquess was nowhere to be seen. It transpired that he had gone to Bath to conduct some business having to do with his father's estates. Sally was immediately cast down. *She* would not have gone *anywhere* for any reason. Therefore he didn't think of her. Therefore what was the use? She was worried, miserable, hurt, and rejected. But she could not leave.

The snow had stopped falling and lay deep and crisp and even over the landscape. The stone tigers on the steps waved their snowy paws ridiculously in the air. More guests began to arrive. Servants bustled backward and forward throughout the great house. Soon an orchestra could be heard rehearsing the inevitable waltz, and Sally's misery soon changed to an almost sick feeling of excitement as the hour of the ball drew nearer. In her heart of hearts, she knew that this was to be her one and only night. She could not stay for the meet in the morning. Lady

Cecily would need to return to London and change into Sally Blane, who would then need to transform herself into Aunt Mabel and return to the palace, sitting with rubber wrinkled hands folded while the love of her life no doubt got down on one knee and proposed to another female.

Miss Fleming and Sally helped each other dress, and both were ready a full half hour before it was time to descend to the ballroom.

"How do I look?" asked Sally breathlessly.

"Very well," said Miss Fleming gruffly. "Very well indeed."

Privately she thought Sally looked very dainty and pretty. Her white silk ball gown had a deep décolletage and was tied with jaunty bows like little wings on the shoulders. It was swept back in a small bustle, and the hem was thickly encrusted with pearls and silver thread.

Her proud little head rose above the collar of pearls. "I bought you something," said Miss Fleming. "How could I have forgotten! Wait a minute."

She rummaged in a large portmanteau and came up with a long silver box, which she opened. Out came a delicate spray of white silk roses, and, brushing aside Sally's stammered thanks, Miss Fleming proceeded to arrange them deftly in the glossy coronet of Sally's hair.

Miss Fleming herself looked very imposing in purple taffeta edged with sable. "It's begun to snow again," she said, looking out of the window. "No hunt tomorrow."

"Oh, then we could stay another day!" cried Sally.

Miss Fleming shook her feathered head. "Why prolong the agony?" she said with a shrug. "Just think, Sally. I mean, he's not going to forgive you if you tell him the truth. To think anything else is sheer fantasy."

A mulish look crossed Sally's pretty face, and she compressed her lips tightly.

This was to be Sally's first ball. There was surely nothing else quite so exciting in a young girl's life as that first descent into the ballroom down the red-carpeted stairs, with the major-domo calling her name like the recording angel from the landing above. As Sally moved sedately down, the mixed smell of hothouse flowers, perfume, powder, macassar oil, cigars, wine, and French cooking rose to meet her like some heady incense burned before the altar of vanity fair.

To Sally's dismay there was no sign of the marquess. Worse—her little silver dance card with its elegant silver pencil was being filled up quickly. In despair, she dived behind a pillar and wrote the name Mr. Grumpit in the space for the supper dance and in the space for the last dance.

She danced and danced, trying to convince herself that she was having a marvelous time, while all the while her large eyes stared over her partners' shoulders, hoping to see the marquess arrive.

And then all at once he was there. Sally had just finished a noisy set of the lancers with Peter Firkin when she found the marquess at her elbow, sleek and groomed and elegant in evening dress. She looked up and caught the glow in his eyes, and all her worries melted away.

The marquess had indeed thought about Sally quite a lot, but in a much simpler and less agonized way than Sally had thought about him. As far as he was concerned, he had enjoyed kissing her and meant to do it again, as soon as possible.

He frowned over her card. "Curst snow," he muttered. "Every single dance taken."

Sally smiled up at him. "I think I could persuade Mr. Grumpit to let you have his dances."

His face lit up with laughter, and he wrote his name quickly over the fictitious Mr. Grumpit's. "I'm sure Mr. . . . er . . . Grumpit won't mind at all," he said. "In fact, this is the supper dance, and I am going to take you onto the floor right now, just in case such a person actually exists."

"Now, you don't think I made him up?" teased Sally, too happy to be embarrassed as she felt his gloved hand at her waist.

He piloted her expertly through the swirling dancers. "No, of course you didn't make him up," he said. "I can see Mr. Grumpit now. He has a gray mustache and a monocle . . ."

"And a red face." said Sally, laughing.

"And he loves you very much."

Sally pretended to be shocked. "Mr. Grumpit loves his wife," she protested.

"Nonsense. He is burning with a secret passion, and having kissed you once, wants to kiss you again."

"Are we talking about Mr. Grumpit?" asked Sally, suddenly breathless.

He smiled down into her flushed face and held her closer. "Of course," he murmured. "And you must never kiss anyone but Mr. Grumpit, for he is very jealous."

Sally swayed in his arms, deaf and blind to everything else. All at once a small hope began to grow in her mind. Perhaps she could tell him the truth after all. While they were at supper.

Now, supper should have been a romantic occasion, seated at one of the many little tables in the candlelight, snow falling outside the long windows, firelight joining the candlelight on the painted walls, but it wasn't. Perhaps it was because the marquess seemed distracted; perhaps it was because Sally was tense, summoning up courage to tell him the truth; or perhaps simply because the palace food was up to its usual standard. Sally wondered desperately where the delicious smell of French cooking had been coming from. The staff dinner?

Everything on her plate seemed to be a hundred years old, from the stale lobster patties to the tough and athletic quail.

At last the marquess turned his blue gaze on her. "I'm afraid we will have no meet tomorrow, Lady Cecily," he said. "It's snowing much too hard."

Sally looked up at him from under her long eyelashes. "Would you be very shocked if I told you I did not know how to ride?" she asked abruptly.

"Well, it's a hypothetical question, since I have had ample evidence that you can ride beautifully. But, yes, of course I would be very much shocked. For it would mean you had lied to me. I cannot bear to be lied to. There is nothing worse, in my opinion, than someone who pretends to be other than they are. It's getting away from the subject of riding a bit, but there was this chap once came to stay here. Father had met him at his club. Said his name was James Harrison, the famous African explorer. Well, he stayed and stayed and stayed. He was always waiting for 'his man to arrive with funds,' and Mother ordered Worthing—the secretary, you know—to let him have ready cash when he needed it. He never seemed to want to talk of his adventures.

" 'Oh, you don't want to hear me boring on about Africa,' he would say. He was very charming and witty, and everyone adored him. The ladies did, anyway, and, as for Mother, she was simply enchanted. But then various little objects began to disappear: a piece of china here and a miniature there. Mother suddenly became suspicious and hired a private detective. It turned out that this chap was actually called Harry Snyder, a well-known confidence trickster. I was all for having him arrested, but Father and Mother— well, typical—they didn't want anyone to know how they had been tricked, and so he got away with it.

"But I tell you this." He leaned across the table, gazing into Sally's wide and startled eyes. "If I ever come across another one, another fake, male or female, I'll simply call the police, no matter who it is. . . . Why are you looking at me like that?"

"Like what?" asked Sally, hurriedly lowering her eyes.

"I don't know, almost as if you were about to say good-bye to me." He gave a light laugh. "You make me feel as if I am standing on a liner, watching you on the shore."

"If you will forgive me for saying so," said Sally, "I think your cook is a confidence trickster."

"Pretty awful, isn't it?" he said, and Sally was glad that her statement about the cook had stopped the marquess from looking at her so intently.

He began to tell her a series of amusing anecdotes about the palace cook, and Sally hardly heard a word.

She could never tell him her real identity now. All she had was this one evening. She would not even come back as Aunt Mabel. Better to make a clean break.

"You're not listening to a word I'm saying."

Sally looked at him in dismay. "I'm—sorry," she stammered. "I—I w-was th-thinking of something else."

"You know," he said, looking at her curiously, "I keep feeling there's some dark mystery about you. Never mind. Your turn to do the talking. Tell me about Africa."

Sally blushed red, thinking of the confidence trickster. "I don't want to talk about it," she said. "I had a bad time there."

The strains of the music filtered into the supper room. "My next partner will be waiting for me," said Sally, getting to her feet. She was all at once glad to escape. She *looked* glad to escape, and by now the marquess's interest was definitely caught. Women were not in the habit of fleeing from him.

He found himself becoming more and more intrigued by the minute with Lady Cecily.

Sally wondered whether she should run away before the last dance, but the thought of being held in the marquess's arms one more time was too much for her. And so at last she was being held by him as they moved to the sugar-sweet strains of *The Merry Widow* waltz. Sally forced the days ahead out of her mind. Only this moment existed. Nothing was real for her but the tall man who held her closely against him. Faces were a blur, gowns and jewels a swirling colored background to her happiness. She had never felt so elated in her life before. At last the magic dance was over. Faces swam back into focus: Mrs. Stuart with her eyes glittering strangely as she looked at her husband; the duchess, fatigued; Miss Wyndham and Peter Firkin standing shoulder to shoulder and looking radiant; and the duke, morose. And there was Miss Fleming waiting to tell Cinderella that the ball was over and it was time to turn into Aunt Mabel again.

Sally stood next to the marquess as the orchestra played the National Anthem. As the last chord was struck he whispered to her, "Let's go for a walk in the snow," and with shining eyes, Sally nodded her head.

"I'll fetch my mantle," she whispered back. "Where shall I meet you?"

"In the conservatory. In half an hour."

Sally nodded, and then he left her side to go and chat with some other guests.

Sally hurried up the stairs, anxious to get her mantle and escape before Miss Fleming should find out what she was up to. For that lady showed an alarming tendency to behave like the chaperon she was pretending to be, and Sally felt sure she would try to stop her going by pointing out all those distressing things, such as it being better to make a clean break.

She slipped quietly down the stairs, grateful that she, as Aunt Mabel, had acquired such good knowledge of the geography of the vast house, that she did not have to look for a servant and ask for directions to the conservatory.

She pushed open the door quietly and stood just inside, her eyes searching the darkness.

The conservatory had been built onto the back of the great house some time in the last century and was, in daylight, Sally remembered, rather like a miniature crystal palace.

But in the hot, humid darkness it seemed mysterious and vast with huge palm trees soaring up to the glass roof.

"Are you there?" she whispered into the blackness—and then let out a squeak of alarm as a pair of strong arms folded about her from behind.

"Darling," the marquess murmured in a low voice, turning her around to face him.

Sally could feel her bones beginning to melt as she felt her body pressed closely against him. Her mantle, which she had been carrying over one arm, fell unheeded to the floor.

And then his lips came down on hers, burning this time, and exploring, causing dizzying skyrockets to burst in her brain. His mouth left hers and began to wander over her face, kissing her closed eyelids, the tip of her nose, her ears, and her neck.

In a tiny corner of Sally's brain alarm bells were beginning to ring. Thoughts jumbled one over the other. She was alone with him without a chaperon. He was kissing her only because she had appeared easy game. His hand left her waist and slid down the low front of her dress, cupping her bosom in a warm clasp.

"No!" cried Sally, wrenching herself free. "You mustn't . . . you frighten me!"

There was a short silence, and Sally could almost sense his anger. Then he said lightly, "We are supposed to be walking in the snow. This tropical atmosphere is having a bad effect on me. Where is your mantle?"

"On the floor," replied Sally in a shaky little voice.

He struck a match and held it up, his face looking like that of a stranger as it was illuminated by the small flame. "Ah, there it is!" He stooped and retrieved her mantle and blew out the match. He put the mantle about her shoulders and, taking her hand in a firm clasp, led her through the darkness of the conservatory to a small glass door that led out to the garden and lawns, glimmering under their carpet of snow.

He opened the door, and Sally stepped out after him. Romance fled before the impact of the ice-cold air and the realization that she had forgotten to change out of her satin dancing slippers, for the snow was already seeping through the thin material.

Letters from many, many distressed girls ran through Sally's troubled brain: *"I don't know*

*what happened . . . I didn't mean to do it
. . . didn't mean to be bad.*" And Sally remembered her own sympathetic, yet rather detached,
replies. For she had always wondered how any
woman could simply surrender her virginity so
easily. With a new maturity, she realized how
close she had probably come to it herself. He had
released her hand and was walking a little way
ahead of her, through the snow.

Light, glittering flakes were falling and cir-
cling out of a black, black sky. The gas was
turned up in one of the rooms above, throwing
a sudden yellow rectangle of light across the
lawn.

"You aren't wearing a coat," Sally called after
the marquess, but he walked on, his head bent,
his hands behind his back, like some royal per-
sonage walking forward to lay another boring
foundation stone.

*My pride would not normally let me run after
any man like this,* thought Sally, rather angrily,
*but it's our last short time together, and he's spoil-
ing it all by stalking off in a temper like that.*

She hurried after him, up to her ankles in
snow, holding up her pearl-embroidered skirts.
She almost collided with him as he came to an

abrupt halt. He tucked her hand in his arm and said, "Let's walk to the rotunda."

Sally nodded, deliriously happy again. The rotunda gleamed against the whiter snow. Sally raised her skirts higher as the snow, away from the shelter of the house, grew deeper. Besotted as she was, she was conscious of a faint feeling of irritation, since he showed no concern for the fact that she was laboring through the winter landscape in a thin pair of evening slippers. He had gone quiet again, preoccupied.

The marquess was in fact wrestling with a problem. His intelligence and all his emotions were telling him that he had fallen in love with Lady Cecily. There was, therefore, no reason on earth why he should not ask for her hand in marriage. But it was all just too easy. Lady Cecily was of good family, his mother and father would be delighted, and nothing could be more correct. He looked at her sideways out of the corner of his eye. Snowflakes were shining on the white roses in her hair, and her piquant little face was delicately flushed.

He had been in severe danger of going much too far too soon back in the conservatory. But never had a female so assaulted his senses. Never had he wanted to possess a girl as much as he wanted to possess Lady Cecily Trevelyn. He had hardly drunk anything at the ball, so it could not be that. He knew instinctively that she was a virgin, and he was not in the habit of becoming hot and bothered over virgins, let alone respectable, marriageable ones.

They had finally reached the rotunda, and he drew her down onto a marble bench, seeming not to notice that it was covered with two inches of snow.

"Cecily," he began, and then repeated "Cecily" again, for Sally had momentarily forgotten her assumed name.

She turned toward him, her eyes large and questioning in the faint illumination from the expanse of white snow. "I am sorry if I frightened you back there," he said, taking her hands in his. "You have quite a devastating effect on my senses. You have—Oh, dash it all . . . come here and let me kiss you again!"

And without waiting for her reply, he swept her into his arms, kissing her lingeringly, molding her body against his, his searching hands taking the pins from her hair so that it cascaded about her shoulders and the white silk roses tumbled down and lay on the harlequin tiles of the floor of the rotunda.

Gradually as he kissed her and kissed her, Sally could sense suddenly a new tenderness in him . . . and all her defenses crumbled.

She buried her fingers in the crisp black curls at his neck and returned his kisses with all her heart and soul, feeling his hands sliding over her breasts, feeling her body burning like a flame.

At last he drew back and took her small face gently between his long fingers. The sky was paling in the east, and somewhere a cold and sleepy bird let out a mournful chirp.

"I love you with all my heart, Cecily," he said. "When can we be married? How soon?"

Love and passion and dreams and romance fled from her wide gray eyes, to be replaced with such a look of bewilderment and loss that he frowned suddenly. That frown brought the memory of how he could not stand liars or confidence tricksters or people who pretended to be other than they were rushing into Sally's brain. The night had gone, her one, precious night. Reality came flooding back. The snow on the bench had melted and was seeping through her coat and gown. Her feet were two blocks of solid ice. Her mantle had been pulled down, exposing her naked shoulders, and the chill wind of dawn brushed its cold fingers over her bared breasts and bruised lips.

"I'm cold, so very cold," whispered Sally, arranging her gown and pulling her mantle with its sealskin collar high around her throat.

He gave her an impatient shake. "I'm asking you to marry me," he said.

Sally rose slowly to her feet. "No," she said, oh, so gently, oh, so sadly. "I can't."

The snow had stopped falling. Sally walked from the rotunda and across the glittering snow toward the palace.

"Cecily!" he called after her. *"Cecily!"*

But I'm not Cecily, thought Sally, feeling a terrible lump rising in her throat. *I'm Sally. And I'm a liar.*

The marquess stared after her diminishing figure in disbelief.

He could not believe she was rejecting him. He could not believe she had turned down his offer of marriage. A small flame of anger was growing in him and burning away his heartache. Well, let her see if he cared! Be damned to her!

But there was something so forlorn in the

droop of her shoulders and the way her fur-edged mantle dragged slowly across the snow behind her.

One more try. *"Cecily!"*

Sally stumbled and nearly fell, amazed at the tearing pain of loss and hurt somewhere below the region of her heart. For one split second she made a small movement, as if her whole soul were about to drag her unwilling body and brain back across the snow to him.

And then she walked on with a sure, quick step. The conservatory door opened and closed.

The marquess felt numb—not with cold. He had an awful feeling he would never see Lady Cecily again.

He did not know that he hadn't even met her.

CHAPTER SIX

By Monday morning the Marquess of Seudenham was reflecting wryly that he could do with a bit of advice from Aunt Mabel. But that lady had been unaccountably detained in London, "due to poor health."

His mother had shaken her head and written off to say that she would travel to London at the end of the week to visit Aunt Mabel's sickbed. The marquess was not to know the consternation with which that letter was met.

He simply could not get the mysterious Lady Cecily out of his head, and by Tuesday, when he read an item in the social columns saying that Lady Cecily had attended a supper party at Lady Courtland's after just having returned from South Africa and was throwing a masked ball that very night at the town house of her guardians, he decided to catch the train to London and attend that ball himself, invitation or no.

The marquess had managed to slowly get over the fury he had felt at Lady Cecily's refusal of his proposal of marriage. But the resultant feelings of loss and hurt and worry were so painful that at times he longed for his anger to come back again.

The hunt had met on the Saturday, and despite her lack of sleep, he had fully expected to see Lady Cecily among the riders. But the hunt had set out over the snow, and halfway through the day he found he could not bear it any longer and had ridden hard to the palace—only to find she had left.

As the train carrying him to London sped through the wintry landscape, the marquess decided stubbornly that there was some strange reason behind Lady Cecily's rejection. She could not have kissed him like that and been indifferent to him. Perhaps she was engaged to some yob in South Africa? He had never proposed marriage to any woman in his life before, but never for a moment had he been expected to be turned down.

He had been hunted too long on the Marriage Market not to know that his title and his fortune set him high above the rest. He was not a vain man and was unaware of the fact that he was extremely handsome, most of the time putting any female admiration down to his title. Now he began to fret about his appearance like a schoolboy undergoing the first pangs of calf love. Was his face showing wrinkles? He had found one suspiciously gray-looking hair among the thick thatch of his black curls only that very morning. How old was Lady Cecily? Why hadn't he checked the peerage? Was he old enough to be her father? Of course not. And on and on his thoughts ran to the thudding of the wheels.

He had a slim town house, which he hardly ever used, in Half Moon Street in Mayfair, since he preferred the country to the town. He looked around it now with new eyes, anxious eyes. How stale and lifeless it seemed. Not a feminine touch anywhere.

He startled his servants by demanding that flowers be arranged in all the rooms and that new curtains be put up to replace the dark velvet hangings. "What kind of curtains, my lord?" My lord did not know. My lord simply knew he wanted something . . . well . . . bright and *pretty*. And the place was freezing. Fires in every room.

Had she been too cold? Good God! He had kept her out half the night in the freezing cold! She must think him a callous monster. In his mind's eye, Lady Cecily changed from the courageous, the sparkling, and the independent Cecily to a young girl who ought to be sheltered from the cares of the world.

He tried to pass the afternoon at his club, among the thick pile carpets and leather armchairs and all the subdued hush of that well-run establishment, which he had always found soothing at the worst of times. But now it irked him. The sleeping figures of two of the older members alarmed him. He might end up like them! Snoring his life away with no wife and children waiting for him at home. Then he remembered it was a masked ball and that he hadn't got a mask, and so he set off to look for one.

He also remembered that Peter Firkin was engaged now to Miss Wyndham, and sickeningly happy, and so he spent some time on Old

Bond Street, choosing an engagement present and settling at last on an enormous box of solid gold knives and forks, and then feeling that it was all too vulgar and ostentatious the minute he had paid for it.

By evening he felt depressed and exhausted and realized he had hardly had any sleep since the day Lady Cecily had left.

He summoned his valet and was helped into his evening clothes. He slipped a black velvet mask into his pocket and set out for the Earl and Countess of Hammering's town house in Kensington.

He did not want to waste time over an argument at the door, so he simply presented his visiting card and said he had lost his invitation, and the magic of his title worked as it had done so many times in the past.

He left his heavy fur-lined cloak and his hat, cane, and gloves downstairs, donned his mask, and mounted the stairs to the ballroom on the first floor.

Here the marquess met his first setback. The earl and countess gracefully accepted his apology for gate-crashing their ward's ball, but looked extremely puzzled when he said he had had the pleasure of dancing with Lady Cecily at his mother's ball.

"You must be mistaken," said Lady Harrington. "Little Cecily has not been out anywhere in England until this evening." The marquess then inquired after their health and said he was sorry to hear they had both been indisposed. That information was met with two blank stares.

"We shall chat later," said the countess firmly, since she had obviously decided the marquess was mad or drunk or both. "I must welcome the other guests. You will find little Cecily in the ballroom."

Bemused, the marquess left them and made his way into a large room full of masked guests. His eyes raked around the long room. Although she would be masked, he was sure he could tell her easily from any other woman in the room. But nowhere could he see that familiar figure or that light cloud of nut-brown hair.

"Well, Paul," said a jovial voice at his elbow. "See old Peter Firkin's got himself engaged." He swung around and stared at the masked face next to his own, recognizing one of his old friends, Stuffy Bingles-Farnworth, by the brush of red hair standing on top of his head.

"Hallo, Stuffy," said the marquess, his eyes still roving around the room. "Looks as if all us old bachelors are beginning to fall like ninepins. Still looking for an heiress?"

"Still looking," said Stuffy gloomily. "Thought I'd try my hand with Lady Cecily, but I'm not *that* desperate."

The marquess swung and faced him, his eyes like two chips of blue ice behind his mask. "*I* think Lady Cecily is the most charming, most fascinating girl I have ever met," he said in a repressive voice.

"Eh, what?" Stuffy stared at the marquess in surprise.

"Where is she anyway?" demanded the marquess. "I can't see her."

"Why, over there!" said Stuffy. "Dancing with that long drip of a fellow, Harry Crompton."

The marquess followed his gaze. Harry Crompton was performing a lively polka. The girl in his arms had frizzy sandy hair and a virulent pink mask.

"That's not Lady Cecily," said the marquess.

"None other," said Stuffy. "And she ought to

wear a mask the whole time—and a gag—if you ask me."

The marquess waited impatiently until the polka was finished. He approached the girl in the pink mask. "Lady Cecily," he said hesitantly. "May I have this dance?"

"Oooh! *Yeth!*" said Lady Cecily. "Very few people have asked me to danth," she confided, "and *I* think its rotten of them, cos it's *my* ball!"

Bewildered, he took her in his arms for the waltz. She concentrated on her steps, counting to three in a loud voice, occasionally crunching down on his foot and then saying "Sowwy," bursting into peals of shrill laughter.

He guided her carefully behind a bank of hothouse flowers. "What are we doing heah?" said Lady Cecily, giggling. "Do you want to kith me?"

"No," he said, removing his mask. "I just want you to remove your mask a minute."

"You *do* want to kith me. Wicked man!"

With many titters and giggles, she removed her mask. Well, handsome is as handsome does, and we can't all be pretty, but there is something rather infuriating when a really plain girl thinks she is a mixture of Venus, Cleopatra, and Lillie

Langtry. Little, pale piggy eyes with white lashes ogled up at him, great rabbit teeth sprouted out from between thin lips, and, under the piled-up fuzz of her sandy hair, her ears stuck out like jug handles. "The twouble is," said Lady Cecily, "I'm iwwesistible!"

"Quite," said the marquess hurriedly. "Oh, *please* put your mask on again, Lady Cecily," he added with such urgency that she began to pout horribly.

"My dear Seudenham," said an acid voice in his ear. "What are you doing with my little Cecily?"

He turned around. Bosom heaving, the Countess of Hammering stood glaring at him awfully.

The marquess opened his mouth to explain about the fake Lady Cecily and closed it again. "I don't know," he said, and before either ward or countess could reply, he strode away across the polished ballroom floor.

He refused to think. His mind was a numb blank. He ordered his carriage and stood impatiently on the red-carpeted steps under the striped awning, waiting for it to be brought around. It had started to snow again, great white flakes drifting past the globes of gaslight from the streetlamps. "She should have come on the hunt," he thought suddenly. "It didn't snow on Saturday." And then his mind went blank again.

It was only when he walked into his town house and into his small sitting room and looked around at the bright flowers and new curtains and crackling fire that he realized that in some mad way he had dreamed of bringing her back with him. If she had been there, which she had not.

For whoever she was, she was not Lady Cecily Trevelyn. She was a liar and an imposter, and he had told her he could abide neither. So he would never see her again.

Which was just as well.

Wasn't it? . . .

Sally sat in a first-class compartment, waiting for the train to Bath to leave the station. She was dressed as Aunt Mabel once more. Mr. Barton's instructions had been short and precise after he had read the letter from the duchess, threatening to visit Aunt Mabel's sickbed. Sally was to return to Banjahar and rid herself of the duchess once and for all, and Mr. Barton did not care how she did it.

At first Sally had protested, but Mr. Barton had held firm. She was by now too valuable an asset to risk exposure. Sally had thought of little else but the marquess since she had returned to London, but with new maturity she felt sure that so long as she did not see him again, she would manage to get over him, or rather not suffer the longing and hurt with such intensity. Time, it is said, cures all, and Sally was prepared to grit her teeth and give it a lot of time. But now she would shortly be seeing him again.

She had the compartment to herself. The train was about to leave any minute. Sally decided to indulge in her latest terrible vice. She opened her reticule cautiously and extracted a box of Turkish cigarettes. She had just lit one and was relaxing in her corner when the guard outside on the platform blew his whistle, and at the same time the compartment door was wrenched open and the Marquess of Seudenham tumbled in.

He threw his portmanteau on the rack and turned and smiled down at the old lady in the corner, who was staring up at him through a cloud of smoke.

184

"Aunt Mabel!" he exclaimed in surprise.

Sally nervously stubbed out her cigarette in the ashtray, burning her gloves in the process, and smiled weakly back. "My nerves, my lord," she said, much flustered. Sally felt sure that little old ladies did not smoke cigarettes.

He stood looking down at her thoughtfully for what seemed a very long time, and Sally dropped her eyes. Then he sank into the corner seat opposite. Sally became aware that the train had left the station.

"So you are going to Banjahar," he said lightly. "Good. We all need your advice."

"I am going for the last time, my lord," said Sally. "It is really most inconvenient."

"Especially when you have been ill," he said with warm sympathy. "You should not let Mother bully you. She doesn't really need you for anything now. By the way, Miss Wyndham and Peter are engaged."

"Splendid!" said Sally without much enthusiasm. What was Hecuba to her or she to Hecuba? How could she share in Miss Wyndham's joy when her own heart was breaking? "And what about you, my lord?" she could not resist asking.

"Ah! That is a painful story. I am in love with an adventuress."

"Oh!"

"Is that all you have to say, wise Aunt Mabel? Oh? Yes, I met a young lady at the ball who pretended to be Lady Cecily Trevelyn. I was quite enchanted. I proposed marriage. She refused. I pursued her to London and found the real Lady Cecily was someone entirely different. I shall probably never see her again, and I'm better off without her. I don't like liars."

"Oh," said Sally again in a dismal voice. After a silence punctuated by the rattling of the train wheels across the points, Sally said, "Perhaps this adventuress was not really so bad. I mean, did she steal anything?"

"No."

"Well, then . . ."

"Really, Aunt Mabel, one can carry understanding too far. Perhaps she meant to steal the family jewels. What other reason could she have for impersonating Lady Cecily?"

"Perhaps she simply wanted to gate-crash the ball," said Sally reasonably, although she did not feel at all reasonable.

Fireworks seemed to be bursting all over her

brain, and for the first time in her life she wondered if she were going to faint from excess of emotion, from warring feelings of hopelessness and elation.

"She's probably not worth bothering about," said the marquess in a flat voice. "I must have been mad."

He took out a copy of the *Times*, shook out its crisp pages, and began to read.

Sally stared sightlessly out at the white winter landscape. Damn and blast Aunt Mabel! She hated her. She hated the marquess for having taken all that precious love and for having thrown it so callously out of his mind.

The newspaper rattled, and one blue eye peered at her around the edge of it.

"I say, Aunt Mabel, I'm being awfully rude. Do you mind if I read the paper?"

"Not at all," said Sally in a dull voice. "It will take your mind off kissing and canoodling."

"Exactly." He laughed, retreating behind the newspaper again.

He was soon engrossed in a letter from a Colonel Henry Mapleson, who was complaining about the practice in the courts of kissing the

Bible and cited the case of an eminent prima donna.

> "The Book, which was handed to her to kiss, was dirty and ill-smelling. Some days after, the lady in question was troubled with a rash on her mouth and chin, which finally affected her throat. The doctor pronounced it a malignant itch, and he felt no hesitancy in declaring it to have been transmitted to his patient through the foul Testament she had been compelled to kiss at the Court."

The Marquess read on, but somewhere in a corner of his brain a little voice nagged, *"Kissing and canoodling." That's what Father said when he saw me kissing that impostor.*

He gave his head a slight shake and read the colonel's summing up.

> "Witnesses in English Courts should take the law in their own hands and refuse to kiss filthy and unclean books, rather than run the risk of catching a cutaneous disease, or something worse.

Your obedient servant,
Henry Mapleson."

But it *was* strange that Aunt Mabel had used the same words. Perhaps . . . just perhaps . . . his mysterious lady had written to Aunt Mabel for advice.

He lowered the paper slowly and stared curiously at Aunt Mabel. With a great roar and whoop the train plunged into a tunnel. It was a short one, and they were soon clattering out into the blinding white of the snowy countryside, which lit up Aunt Mabel's face in sharp relief. How young her eyes were! And how remarkably like that girl's! He was going mad. He was being haunted. He had a feeling that the love of his life was staring at him from behind a wrinkled mask. Then the embankment reared up outside the window, casting the compartment into shadow, and Aunt Mabel was once again very much Aunt Mabel.

She lowered her eyes before his scrutiny and, opening her capacious reticule, took out a magenta-colored piece of knitting and proceeded to mangle away at it in a surprisingly inexpert manner.

"What are you knitting?" asked the marquess.

"A scarf," said Sally, looking down hopefully at the wool in her hands and hoping that that was what it was supposed to be. Miss Frimp had insisted she take knitting with her. Just the right touch, Miss Frimp had said.

"You're not very good at it," observed the marquess, watching her fumbling fingers dropping stitches. "Here, let me."

He held out his hands, and Sally stared at him, aghast. "You can't mean it!" she said. "You surely don't know how to knit!"

"Of course I do," he said cheerfully. "My governess taught me when I was four, and I've never forgotten." He took the mess of wool and needles from her nerveless fingers and studied it with interest.

"I sometimes wonder if you are the sweet old lady you pretend to be," he said, unaware of Sally's start of alarm. "All ladies are supposed to be able to knit."

"I wish you would stop calling me old," said Sally with some asperity. "I am not yet in my grave, and you are not exactly a spring lamb yourself."

"Tut-tut. Temper, temper. Look. I have to

pull out these rows. It's plain knitting. Very simple. Now, if you watch me . . ."

"I don't want to watch you," said Sally pettishly. "You look stupid. Men don't knit."

"Yes, they do. You should be grateful to me for enlarging your experience. And it's no use glaring at me. I find this very therapeutic."

He proceeded to knit away expertly, the steel knitting needles flying in his long fingers.

Sally gave a little gasp. The white, vacant face of the Honorable Freddie Stuart was staring in the door from the corridor. He screwed his monocle more firmly in his eye and opened the door.

The marquess looked up with irritation. He found to his surprise that he did not want to be interrupted. He wanted to be alone with Aunt Mabel. He was about to analyze this strange feeling when he became aware at the same time that Freddie was goggling at him.

"'Lo, Freddie," said the marquess. "Still staying with us?"

"Yes," said Freddie, glaring openly at the knitting. "Been to see my doctor. Got pains in the tum-tum."

"Wife poisoning you again?" asked the marquess, deftly beginning another row.

"No. Your father's cook. Food's a disgrace."

"Then, why don't you take yourself off?" demanded the marquess crossly. "You've been with us for weeks and weeks."

Now, Freddie and his wife had made an art of living on anyone they could. Mostly they were moved on after a couple of weeks, but the duke and duchess had shown no sign of giving them their marching orders, and Freddie was prepared to put up with the worst cooking in the world just so long as it was free.

"Never mind that," said Freddie crossly. "What you knitting for?"

"Because I like it," said the marquess placidly.

"It's effeminate."

"Rubbish. I'm helping the war effort."

"What war?"

"What a lot of stupid questions you do ask. Haven't you got a compartment of your own? There's a terrible draft and it's either coming from that door, which you so stupidly left open, or it's coming from your mouth, which is hanging open. So why don't you be a good chap and shut both."

"It's no use trying to insult me," said Freddie.

The marquess stopped his knitting and smiled nicely. "Oh, I found that out long ago. I shall put it in simple English. Go away. I want to be alone with Aunt Mabel. I love her madly."

Freddie turned his astonished gaze on Sally. "But she's old enough to be your mother."

"Age is no barrier," said the marquess placidly. He began to knit again.

I have fallen in love with a madman, thought Sally wildly. *He will turn out just like his father.*

Freddie backed out of the compartment. "Wait till I tell the fellows at the club," he jeered.

"Tell them," said the marquess, "and I'll tell them about you and Flossie Jenkins on Boat Race night. The things you can get up to in a punt. Dear me!"

Freddie fled, slamming the compartment door.

"Thank goodness," said the marquess. "It's snowing again. I don't mean 'thank goodness it's snowing again.' I mean 'thank goodness I got rid of that idiot'."

"You were very rude," said Sally severely. "What about my reputation?"

"My dear Aunt Mabel! A Bible-bashing lady like yourself is above the petty sneers of the common man."

"Has it ever occurred to you that you are eccentric?" asked Sally curiously.

His fingers flew over the wool. "Eccentric? No. I'm a very ordinary chap. Oh, you mean the knitting? Well, it keeps my mind off that wretched girl I'm in love with, and I never really care what people think of me anyway."

He blinked before Sally's sudden dazzling smile.

As far as Sally was concerned, he could knit until doomsday. He had said he loved her.

"The train's slowing," she said, rubbing at the window with her hand. "Oh, dear!"

"Oh, dear what?"

"I can't seem to see a thing."

He put down his knitting and leaned across her to look out through the cleared space she had made in the condensation on the glass.

"It's snowing a blizzard. What odd weather! It's only the beginning of December. We don't usually get weather like this until February. And

194

this is one of the worst blizzards I can remember. Why don't you join me in the dining car? It's about time for lunch."

Sally gladly agreed, for his proximity as he leaned over her was doing strange things to her senses.

They made their way along the corridor of the train, which was only creeping along through the roaring, blinding snowstorm.

Sally felt suddenly shy as she faced the marquess across the small table, with its snowy napkin and little lace-covered table lamp, in the dining compartment. "I thought you would have your own carriage and dining room," she said.

"No. I don't bother with that unless I'm taking a lot of guests down for the weekend. Now, we're going to have a lot to drink and go back to the compartment and sleep like logs, because it's going to take us absolutely hours to get to Bath."

So he ordered sherries for them before the meal, a good bottle of hock with the fish, a surprisingly excellent Château Lafite with the braised filet of mutton, a bottle of sauterne with the Nesselrode pudding, and port with the Stilton, and he entertained Sally throughout the meal by inventing mad letters from fictitious readers and demanding her replies.

The dining car gradually emptied, other passengers staring curiously at the giggling old lady and the handsome young man.

When they finally went back to their compartment, the train gave a great protesting lurch, a high dismal whistle, and came to a stop.

The marquess took out his handkerchief and rubbed the window. The train had stopped between the shelter of two high embankments.

"Wait here," said the marquess, "and I'll find out what has happened."

After a short time he was back. "I'm afraid we can't go any further. On the other side—out of the shelter of these embankments—the line's completely blocked. There is no heating. We are stranded here until the storm stops and someone digs us out."

"What shall we do?" asked Sally.

"Sleep," he said curtly. He sat down beside her after lifting his heavy fur coat down from the rack. "We'll put this over us and be snug as bugs."

He suited the action to the words and slid an

arm around Sally with easy familiarity, feeling the little old lady's body begin to tremble slightly.

"You're cold," he said, rubbing her shoulders sympathetically while Sally bit back a moan. "There! Just lean back on my shoulder and you'll soon be as warm as anything."

It was fortunate for Sally that she had drunk so much at lunchtime. Despite all the tumultuous and disturbing emotions his proximity aroused in her, Sally soon fell into a heavy sleep.

The marquess held Aunt Mabel's slim body against his own, feeling a surge of affection for this strange old lady who did not behave like an old lady at all, and who had an enchanting, infectious laugh, just like a young girl's.

He awoke briefly as a railway official came in to light the oil lamp, and then drifted off to sleep again, lulled by the noise of the storm.

When he at last awoke completely it was to find that the storm had apparently ceased and that the train was slowly moving forward again.

Faint smells of food were drifting in from the nearby dining car, and the marquess found to his amazement that he was feeling hungry again. His mouth felt dry and sour after all he had drunk at luncheon. He gave Aunt Mabel a little shake, and she came awake immediately, looking up at him through her spectacles with those large, youthful gray eyes, which were so like the eyes of the mysterious girl who had gate-crashed his mother's home and had stolen nothing valuable except his heart.

Dinner was a silent affair. The marquess's senses seemed to be picking up a strange feeling of unease from Aunt Mabel, and he remembered that the old dear had had quite a crush on him on her visit and probably still had. Amazing! He wondered how old she was. She was so very, very wrinkled, and her skin had a dead and lifeless look. Only her eyes seemed young.

By silent consent they drank very little at dinner. Neither felt like talking, and it was a very subdued pair who eventually returned to the compartment.

The marquess resumed his knitting, and Sally asked him to lift down her suitcase for her, and, extracting a bundle of letters and a notebook, she proceeded to work on her correspondence.

The train did not lurch into Bath station until one in the morning. The roads to the palace were blocked, and the inns and hotels were full. In despair, the marquess at last found a room for them at the Pelican, an old coaching inn on the outskirts of town, and returned to the station, where he had left Aunt Mabel in front of the fire in the ladies' waiting room, to tell her the good news.

"One room," exclaimed Sally faintly.

"I had to say you were my mother," explained the marquess. "For Heaven's Sake, behave like a sensible woman. We must have somewhere to sleep. I am tired and stiff, and I am damned if I am spending the night in this station."

"But surely they know your mother?"

"No. New management. Hurry up and stop staring at me. We've got to walk, and it's quite a way. I'll help you as much as I can."

Sally meekly allowed herself to be helped through the snow-covered streets, reflecting that she would have needed his help even if she had been allowed to behave in a manner befitting her *real* age. The snow had frozen into high, powdery drifts, creating a frozen world, a white, mysterious world, through which they moved silently. The hems of Sally's dress and mantle were becoming soaked despite the light, powdery snow, and her feet were absolutely frozen.

At last they reached the Pelican, which had been built around the seventeenth century and was full of stairs up and stairs down, Toby jugs, armor, and old-world objets d'art made in Birmingham in the hope of attracting some of those American tourists who were supposed to like that sort of thing. The Pelican was originally a coaching inn, but its trade had been taken away by the railway.

Sally was treated with all the deference given to a duchess, although the landlord, who had been about to offer Her Grace tea, was somewhat startled when the marquess said firmly that his mother would like a bottle of brandy sent up to her room.

The marquess had sent one of the inn servants back to the station to collect their suitcases and suggested they sit in front of the fire until their belongings arrived.

Sally was now feeling sleepy again and nervous at the same time.

The room was very small, shadowed, and cosy, lit by a pair of candles stuck in brass candlesticks on the high velvet-draped mantel. The bed was a four-poster and very small, either having been made in an age when the average Briton was stunted, or when they preferred to sleep bolt upright like the French aristocracy to prevent congestion of the lungs.

Sally slowly swirled the brandy around in her glass, reflecting that she had drunk enough since she left London to last a lifetime.

The brandy on top of all she had had before took immediate effect, and her sleepiness increased, while her nervousness began to ebb a little.

"Where will you sleep, my lord?" asked Sally, staring at the leaping flames of a small coal fire.

"Here, of course."

"Here! Where? In the chair?"

"Don't be silly. In bed."

Well, he was paying for the room, after all. "Then I shall sleep in my chair," said Sally.

"Aunt Mabel," he said testily. "I know you are very young at heart, but at times you are ridiculous. I must remind you that you are old enough to be my grandmother, and my intentions toward you are strictly honorable. We shall both share the bed, just as I would do with my own mother, old as I am, if she should find herself in the same predicament."

"Of course," said Sally hurriedly. "I didn't think—didn't mean—"

"Oh, then what did you think and mean?"

"I don't know," said Sally stupidly. "I'm tired."

The servant arriving with their luggage stopped conversation for a while. Then the marquess rose to his feet. "I shall leave you to change, Aunt Mabel. I shall go downstairs and wander about. Don't be long."

When he left the room Sally fairly scrambled out of her clothes and into a long flannel nightgown that buttoned high to the throat and had long tight sleeves.

The heat from the fire did not seem to reach as far as the bed, and the sheets felt icy-cold. Some thoughtful servant had put a stone hot water bottle at the foot of the bed, but it was as red-hot as the bed was icy, and Sally almost burned her feet. She lay staring up at the chintz bed canopy until the marquess returned. He entered the room quietly, without looking at the bed, and blew out the candles. She closed her eyes tightly, hearing the rustle as he undressed.

The bed creaked as he climbed in, and she moved as far to the edge as she could.

"Good night, Aunt Mabel," came a soft, mocking voice out of the darkness.

"Good night, my lord," replied Sally miserably. What would Aunt Mabel advise a girl to do in this situation? Sally closed her eyes wearily. *If anyone wrote to me about this,* she thought, *telling me that they had pretended to be an old woman and had, due to inescapable circumstances, ended up in bed with the Marquess of Seudenham, pretending to be his mother, I would simply think some poor girl was deranged and tear it up!*

The clock on the mantel gave an asthmatic cough and chimed out four o'clock, and a coal fell on the hearth. But despite her turmoil of emotions, Sally fell asleep, determined to be the first to wake.

However it was the marquess who woke first. He climbed gently from the bed and, walking to the window, opened the curtains. Sun blazed down on a white world. It shone into the little room and onto the face of the sleeping Aunt Mabel.

The marquess looked down at her as she lay sleeping—and then looked closer, his eyes suddenly sharp and suspicious.

The glaring light was shining full on Aunt Mabel's rubber wrinkles, shining *through* them, making them transparent, so that underneath them, like a sleeping beauty, lay the young face of Sally Blane.

He bent closer. At the edge of Aunt Mabel's shaggy eyebrows gleamed a little shining trail.

"Gum arabic," he muttered. She was very heavily asleep. He gently pushed the white wig and stared at the line of soft nut-brown hair exposed underneath.

All at once he knew he had found his impostor. And yet, in some mad way, he *knew* she *was* Aunt Mabel, who answered letters to *Home Chats*. He suddenly could think of several very enjoyable ways of punishing her for her deception, but he decided to behave himself instead and to go out and assess the state of the roads.

By the time Sally descended timidly to the inn dining room, the marquess cheerfully informed her that he had telephoned the palace for a carriage, as the roads were clear. Sally dropped her eyes before his mocking blue gaze. She had put on a hat with a heavy veil, and he watched with great amusement as she tried to eat her breakfast of bacon and eggs without raising it.

204

"That's very decorative," he said at last.

"What is, my lord?"

"Those fascinating little bits of egg and bacon that are sticking to the edge of your veil. Are you trying to set a new fashion?"

"No," Sally mumbled, raising her veil and wondering what had put him in this mood. He seemed extremely elated. His eyes were shining and followed her every movement until she became so nervous that her teeth rattled against her teacup.

Several times she opened her mouth to say something and then closed it again.

When the carriage arrived, he tenderly helped her into it, holding her elbow—it seemed to Sally —in an unnecessarily firm grip.

"How long do you plan to stay?" he asked as the carriage lurched over the snowy ruts.

"As short a time as possible," said Sally. "I mean—I have to get back to London in, say, two days."

"Two days? After all your ordeal in getting here? How can you bear to tear yourself away from my fascinating company so soon?"

"I don't know," mumbled Sally, wondering what had come over him.

205

Suddenly apprehensive, she fished in her reticule and produced a small steel mirror and studied her reflection. The aged face of Aunt Mabel stared back at her.

"You look very well," said the marquess. "Quite the thing. No one would guess from your innocent face, Aunt Mabel, that you had just spent the night in bed with me."

"My lord! *Really!*" Sally threw him such an outraged glance that he was momentarily taken aback and wondered whether he had made some awful mistake. Then he remembered the nut-brown hair under the wig and smiled at her shocked face.

"You are such a charming, fascinating, and irresistible woman," he said, "that you quite turn my poor head."

"You are talking rubbish," said Sally in her most Aunt Mabelish manner. "I liked you better when you were knitting."

He smiled at that, but did not make any more remarks, and to Sally's relief he contented himself with looking out of the window at the passing scene.

Sally snuggled into the carriage rugs, leaned her head back against the squabs, and pretended to go to sleep so as to avoid any further conversation.

But soon pretense became a reality, and she did not awaken until the carriage was crunching over the snowy gravel in front of Banjahar Palace.

Her old room was still there waiting for her. The duchess was mildly glad to see her, but explained that all the problems seemed to have been solved, since Miss Wyndham was not to marry Paul after all. She went on to say that it was such a shame that Aunt Mabel had missed the ball, because Paul had seemed quite smitten with Lady Cecily Trevelyn, who would have been eminently suitable but—alas!—it had come to nothing.

Apart from Sally, the only other house guests this time were the Honorable Freddie and Mrs. Stuart.

Mrs. Stuart was passing through the hall as Sally was following the housekeeper taking Sally up to her room. She bestowed a grotesque wink on Sally, and Sally tried to control a shudder of distaste. The woman was quite mad.

Once in the sanctuary of her sitting room, Sally heaved a sigh of relief. She began to think that she might be able to escape with grace. Instinctively she felt the duchess had lost interest in Aunt Mabel. Even Sally knew that it was quite usual for strange people to be taken up by society. But unless they actually belonged, they were quickly dropped.

The sky outside was turning milky white. Sally looked at it anxiously as she removed her hat. Surely it could not snow again. It was no use staying to be near the marquess when every encounter only made matters worse.

A footman scratched at the door and announced that luncheon was being served in the small dining room.

Sally quickly changed into a depressing gray wool frock with purple embroidery, straightened her wig, and went downstairs with a quickly beating heart.

"My darling," cried the marquess gaily as she entered the dining room. "Come and sit next to me and hold my hand."

The duchess dropped her spoon in her soup and stared at her son with her mouth open. The Honorable Freddie let out a snigger, opened his mouth to comment on the marquess's outlandish behavior on the train, remembered Flossie and Boat Race night, and shut it again.

Sally gingerly sat down next to the marquess, who gently took her hand, turned it over, and pressed a warm kiss into its palm.

"Freud has a name for it," announced the duke from the other end of the table. "Something about pussycats."

"Oedipus complex," snapped Mrs. Stuart.

"I don't like the Greeks," said the duchess, feeling on firm ground. "You never know what they're going to get up to. Now, take Priscilla Forbes-Bennet in Athens in 1902. A waiter! At the Grande Bretagne of all things. Is that what this eddy-thing is about?"

"Not quite," said Mrs. Stuart nastily. "It means you are either in love with your mother or a woman old enough to be your mother."

The duchess sat bolt upright in her chair, rigid with shock and disapproval. "The trouble with all this awful nonsense," she said severely, "is that it appeals to repressed people with minds like sewers. Paul, you are simply behaving like a clown. Aunt Mabel! Drink your soup."

"Yes, Your Grace," said Sally, who had turned quite pink under her wrinkles. She took

a hurried mouthful of Brown Windsor soup—
and choked. The soup was burning hot.

The marquess patted her on the back.

"Can't you keep your hands off her?" asked
the duke, with interest. "I know what it feels
like, dear boy, but it's neither the time nor
place."

Tears of pain and embarrassment started into
Sally's eyes, and the marquess decided she had
suffered enough—for the moment—and turned
to his father and began to talk about the latest
improvements in synthetic fertilizers.

I don't care, thought Sally wildly. *I've got to
escape directly after lunch. He's guessed. Somehow, he's guessed.*

"I say, this soup tastes funny," said the Honorable Freddie plaintively. "I—"

A startled look came onto his face, and he
clutched at his chest while they all stared at him.
An amazed look crossed his face, and with a
little gurgling sound, he dropped his head in his
soup, and his soul rose from the Brown Windsor
and departed to the undiscovered country from
whose bourn no traveler returns.

His monocle sprang from his dead eye and

rolled across the table, glaring up accusingly at Sally, like another disembodied eye.

Sally gripped the arms of her chair quite tightly.

The marquess quickly went around the table and lifted Freddie's head out of the soup and, supporting him, felt for his pulse.

"Mrs. Stuart," he said, "I am afraid Freddie is dead."

"It's his heart. I knew it would happen," said Mrs. Stuart calmly.

Sally was too young to recognize the calm of utter shock and despair. She was outraged. Justice must be done.

The duke rose to his feet. "I'll call Doctor Barchester," he said.

"You'll call the police."

The duke and duchess, the marquess, and Mrs. Stuart all gazed at Aunt Mabel, aghast.

"What?" demanded the duke stupidly, his high color at its most pronounced.

"That woman," said Sally, slowly and distinctly and pointing to Mrs. Stuart, "told me that she intended to poison her husband. She said that Doctor Barchester was too old to be efficient and that he would put 'heart attack' on the certificate if she told him to. I insist that the police be called and that an autopsy be performed on Mr. Stuart."

"Come with me," said the duchess, walking away from the table. Sally followed her out.

The duchess swung around in the hall. "What's all this nonsense?" she demanded. And so Sally told her.

"Annabelle Stuart has been talking that sort of rubbish for years," said the duchess coldly. "You have done a terrible thing to add to her shock and grief with your wicked accusations."

"I believe she poisoned him," said Sally stubbornly.

The duchess surveyed Aunt Mabel with awful contempt. Then she touched a bell on the wall. When the butler answered the summons, Her Grace said in a voice that dripped acid, "This person is leaving, *now.* Have her out of here, bag and baggage, as fast as possible."

Then raking Sally from head to toe with a look of utter disgust, the duchess turned on her heels and marched back into the small dining room, slamming the door behind her.

Sally was more than ever bent on seeing justice done. Her anger against the villainous Mrs.

Stuart kept her at top boil, and she startled the duke's servants by demanding to be set down at the police station in Bath.

Paul, she was sure, had discovered her identity—or rather had recognized under the disguise of Aunt Mabel the girl he had proposed to. He had looked as shocked as the others when she made her accusation. He should discover that she had been right. The police were politely disbelieving, but Aunt Mabel's fame had spread far and wide and at last they were impressed. Sally said she would stay at the Palace Hotel in Bath until she heard the result of the autopsy.

Nonetheless, the police wanted to spare the ducal family as much embarrassment as possible. The matter was kept out of the inky hands of the press, and the autopsy was rushed through. In a bare twenty-four hours an Inspector Davidson called on Aunt Mabel at the Palace Hotel.

Sally listened in horror as he explained that the autopsy, which had been performed by a famous London surgeon, had revealed that the Honorable Freddie Stuart had died of a heart attack, nothing more.

213

Sally buried her face in her hands and burned with shame and distress.

His voice softening a little, the inspector pulled up a chair and sat down opposite her.

"Now look here, mum," he said. "I've no doubt that what you told us was all true—that Mrs. Stuart had told you she was going to poison her husband. But these here people have their strange ways, and Mrs. Stuart has been saying the same thing for years. Even her husband knew. Didn't anyone tell you?"

In despair Sally remembered the conversation in the railway compartment with Freddie, the Marquess blithely asking Freddie if his wife was still trying to poison him.

"Someone s-said s-something," she faltered.

"Ah, well, there you are," said the inspector. "That's the aristocracy for you, mum. Why, if some of us behaved like them, they'd have us locked up for sure. Still, it's not for us to criticize our betters, is it? You've done a cruel and very silly thing, but the family has decided to forgive you, since they can understand you being confused by their little ways."

Little ways! Sally felt she had wandered into a *Through the Looking Glass* world.

All she wanted to do was to get as far away from the lot of them as possible. She would never get over this shame and disgrace. Never.

After the inspector left, she went downstairs to pay her hotel bill. The bill, said the clerk, smiling, had been sent to the Marquess of Seudenham at his lordship's request.

Sally eventually climbed onto the Bath train bound for London, feeling as if the coals of fire that had been heaped on her head were burning through her wig.

CHAPTER SEVEN

"Have some more tea," said Miss Fleming soothingly.

Miss Frimp, Miss Fleming, and Sally were seated around the table in their Bloomsbury flat. Sally had cried until she could cry no more, telling them, when she was able, the whole story of her horrible visit.

"You're well out of it, you know," said Miss Fleming. "You would be amazed at the things I hear when I go down to the country with Mr. Wingles. At the last house party, they were all talking about old Lord Beech's little ways. They said he harnesses his wife up to the dogcart and drives her around the estate."

"Goodness!" screamed Miss Frimp.

"Now, you, Sally," pursued Miss Fleming,

"would be better off married to a nice clean-cut army officer."

"I want Paul," said Sally in a dreary voice.

"Well, you can't have him," said Miss Fleming testily. "You're a very lucky girl. You say he recognized you and didn't expose you? Even after you said all that about Mrs. Stuart? Believe me, you're very lucky indeed. And only think! You're writhing in shame and mortification, and all because you accused that old trout, Annabelle Stuart, of killing her husband. Well, if you ask me, you're not to be blamed. The woman's raving mad. She's been going on like Lady Macbeth for so long that someone was bound to take her seriously. She's got no one to blame but herself. It's all been very painful, but the best thing you can do, Sally, is to start work in the morning and work and work and work. I find that's the best cure for any ill."

"All right," said Sally drearily. "I'll work and work and work, and one of these days I won't need to disguise myself as Aunt Mabel. I'll *look* like Aunt Mabel."

"There's nothing wrong with age," said Miss Frimp severely, and Sally apologized hurriedly, for Miss Frimp did look exactly like Aunt Mabel, except her wrinkles were real.

Sally took herself off to bed but, tired as she was, it was a long time before she fell asleep. The marquess's handsome face and mocking blue eyes seemed to float in front of her in the darkness of the room. She loved him utterly and completely, and he was probably as mad as a hatter. They all were. And with that dismal thought, she at last fell asleep.

A week passed while a brief thaw turned the London streets into miserable canyons of slush. Sally worked and worked, the pain in her heart almost constant. Now she knew why love was described as a sickness. "Love is a sickness full of woes,/All remedies refusing." She was touched by the affection and sympathy of her two elderly friends.

Her distress was not helped by a surprise visit from Emily, who arrived at the Bloomsbury flat one evening with all the children.

Emily was remarkably uninterested in Sally's job or her friends. She simply sat there, large and placid, while her children kicked the furniture and Marmaduke got sick on the carpet. Sally envisaged presenting, as her only family, Emily and offspring at Banjahar, and shuddered. Perhaps she should welcome Emily's visit, yet it surely underlined the vast gulf that lay between her background and that of the marquess. Their father had been a colonel, but his regiment was not one of the famous ones, and his background had been unashamedly middle-class. The social code was strict. Everyone knew that the good Lord placed people in their strata on the day they were born, and to try to climb higher was flying in the face of Providence.

Certainly the aristocracy married actresses and chorus girls, but somehow they did not seem to lose their heads over middle-class girls and, if they did, it was usually to ally themselves with some wealthy American heiress who would save the crumbling family estates from going under the hammer.

Matilda Fleming was very worried about Sally. The girl was not eating enough. Matilda racked her brains to try to remember if she had ever been in love and could not. Her sole aim in life had been to be financially independent. Mr. Wingles, her boss, was a bachelor. She had been his secretary for many years, anticipating his every need, filling in as substitute wife when he was summoned to the newspaper proprieter's estate. She was very fond of him, very fond indeed, she admitted to herself. But her feelings toward him had never blossomed into anything warmer than a sort of maternal affection. So mused Miss Fleming as she stared from her window down into the congested traffic of Fleet Street.

And then she craned forward. A glittering carriage was pulling to a halt a little way up the street but still in her line of vision. As she watched, the Marquess of Seudenham alighted. He looked up and down the street and then started to say something to his coachman on the box.

"Ah, Miss Fleming," said Mr. Wingles, coming out of his office, "if you will just type—"

"Can't!" said Miss Fleming, leaping to her feet and shooting past him at a rate of knots.

He stared after her in amazement. In all the years she had worked for him, he had never even seen her flurried.

Miss Fleming shot out of the office of the *Daily Bugle* and, lifting up her skirts, sprinted up Fleet Street like a six-year-old. The marquess was still talking to his coachman and was fortunately about the only person who did not turn around to watch the strange sight of an elderly lady pelting through the slush as if the hound of Heaven were after her.

Sally jumped to her feet in alarm as Miss Fleming erupted into her office, babbling, "He's here. He's coming here. The marquess."

"What am I going to do?" wailed Sally.

"What's all the row?" demanded Mr. Barton, coming into Sally's office and staring, amazed, at Miss Fleming.

"I think," said Miss Frimp primly, "that Miss Fleming is trying to tell us that the Marquess of Seudenham is coming here to unmask Aunt Mabel."

"Oh, no, he's not," said Mr. Barton, springing into action. "Here, Sally, get into my office, lock the door, and stay there. Miss Fleming—go with her. Miss Frimp—get behind the desk. You're going to be Aunt Mabel and that's that. All our jobs depend on it."

He hustled Sally before him into his office, Miss Fleming following on their heels, ignoring Miss Frimp's frightened cry of protest.

"Oh, please," begged Sally. "He knows I'm

not an old lady. He saw through the disguise. Can't I see him?"

"Look here, my girl," said Mr. Barton sternly, locking Sally and Miss Fleming and himself into his office. "You gave me your promise that no one—I repeat, NO ONE—would ever find out that Aunt Mabel is not the sweet old bird she's cracked up to be, and I'm holding you to that promise. I—"

He broke off as they heard footsteps on the stairs.

"It's him," whispered Miss Fleming. "Shhhh!"

The Marquess of Seudenham was feeling remarkably cheerful. Freddie's funeral had gone off well. Not a breath of scandal had reached the press. Mrs. Stuart had found on the reading of her late husband's will that she had been left a very wealthy woman indeed, and that had gone a long way toward mitigating her grief.

His mother, on calmer reflection, had forgiven Aunt Mabel. "If one didn't know that Annabelle Stuart was practically certifiable, then a mistake like that could arise," his mother had said.

Now all he wanted to do was see the girl he

had held in his arms in the snow. He felt sure she would not wear her disguise in the office.

He stood for a moment on a small, dark, dingy landing. And then he saw the frosted glass door marked LETTERS EDITOR.

He found that his heart was beating hard. He straightened his waistcoat, straightened his tie, opened the door, and walked in.

The room was in semidarkness. Miss Frimp got up and came around the desk. "Can I assist you in any way, sir?" she asked nervously.

The marquess threw back his head and laughed. "Oh, my darling love," he said. "Do you have to wear all that rubbish in the office as well?"

Miss Frimp opened her mouth and let out a small bleating sound. Still laughing, he pulled the old lady into his arms.

"You enchant me," he said, suddenly serious. Then he bent his head and kissed her passionately. All at once he realized he was, in fact, holding an elderly lady in his arms. He released her abruptly and looked at her in dawning horror. "Oh, God, I've made a terrible mistake," he gasped. "My apologies, ma'am." And turning on his heels, he fled out of the door and down the stairs.

Miss Frimp stood, one hand leaning on the desk for support, staring after him. Across the landing, Mr. Barton cautiously unlocked his door.

He waited a few moments before gingerly opening the door of Sally's office. Sally and Miss Fleming followed close behind.

Miss Frimp was still standing where the marquess had left her.

"Are you all right, Miss Frimp?" asked Mr. Barton anxiously. "You look strangely flushed. He—he didn't hit you or anything?"

"He kissed me," said Miss Frimp dreamily, "and . . . and . . . do you know, I *liked* it!"

"Oh!" wailed Sally. "It should have been me!"

The Marquess of Seudenham retired to his country estate, his mind a blank. He tried to lose himself in the intricacies of estate management and farming, which usually kept him totally absorbed. But as the long winter wore on, that wretched girl, whoever she was, began to creep back insidiously into his thoughts. At first sheer humiliation and rage kept him from thinking of her, for he had been made to look an utter fool twice, and for that he put the blame fair and square on "Aunt Mabel's" shoulders.

The bitter cold vanished at last as the spring finally arrived. His mother had telephoned several times, asking him to come home on a visit, and each time he had put her off, always preferring to immerse himself in his own affairs. At last, as the days grew warmer, he began to make several trips up to town to see his friends. Then once again he began asking a select few to go back with him for weekend house parties. The talk was all of the forthcoming Season, but the marquess felt little interest in it. For some reason he felt sure he would not find his adventuress at any of the functions.

It was only when he admitted that she would not leave his thoughts that he finally decided to sit down one day and either exorcise her or find some clue as to her whereabouts.

And so he sat down and wrote as much about "Aunt Mabel" as he knew. As his pencil flew over the paper a strange picture began to emerge.

He sat back and reread what he had written and frowned. He was all at once sure that his lady had, in fact, really been employed as Aunt Mabel and that the old lady he had embraced so passionately had been masquerading as Aunt Mabel to deceive him. Lady Cecily—he still called her that in his mind—was undoubtedly a very young girl. Would it be at all possible that the magazine did not want anyone to know that their famous Aunt Mabel was a young girl?

He took a deep breath and decided to try once more. But this time he would see the editor.

As he mounted the steps of *Home Chats* he was met by the office boy, who laconically informed him that Mr. Barton was in "Auntie's" around the corner. The marquess looked puzzled, his brain full of Aunt Mabel. "Auntie's," explained the office boy, was the Red Lion.

Fortunately for the marquess, the Red Lion was comparatively empty, and the obliging landlord indicated Mr. Barton, who was sitting at a small table in the corner over a pint of beer. His head was bent over a sheaf of notes, and he was writing busily.

His look of surprise when the landlord and the marquess came up to him soon changed to one of trepidation at the sound of the marquess's name.

"Sit down," said Mr. Barton with a sigh. "I suppose you've come about Aunt Mabel, my lord?"

The marquess nodded, ordered a pint of beer, and sat down at the table with Mr. Barton.

"Well, my lord," began Mr. Barton reluctantly. "How can I be of assistance to you?"

"Who is Aunt Mabel?" demanded the marquess.

"The elderly lady you saw on your last visit to our offices? Her real name is Miss Frimp."

The marquess took a deep breath. "Now, I want the truth, Mr. Barton. At the time of Aunt Mabel's visit to my mother, was that Miss Frimp?"

Mr. Barton hesitated.

"The truth, man!"

Mr. Barton spread his hands in an oddly Gallic gesture of resignation.

"No, my lord."

"Then who was she?" The marquess resisted a strong temptation to pick up Mr. Barton and shake the information out of him.

"I suppose since I don't know where she is now, there can be no harm in telling you," said Mr. Barton, taking a pull at his beer.

And so he told the marquess about the death of the original Aunt Mabel, and how the young girl in the crumpled sailor hat had taken over and had been so good at the job that he had employed her on the understanding that no one must ever find out her true identity.

He explained how they were frightened that the duchess would find out that the famous Aunt Mabel was only a young girl and that Sally had disguised herself as an elderly lady.

"But something happened," said Mr. Barton sadly. "Sally suddenly ups and says—let me see, about the end of January, I think—that she doesn't want to go on pretending to be someone she's not. She says she's already trained Miss Frimp, her secretary, how to answer the letters, and she says as how Miss Frimp looks like the picture of Aunt Mabel in the magazine. I still didn't want to let her go. Said she could stay and write another column. But she insisted she had to get away. I don't know why," said Mr. Barton, although he knew precisely why. He knew it was because Sally was in love with the marquess and had come to the conclusion that marriage was out of the question and had decided to remove herself from anything that reminded her of him.

"But you must have her address," said the marquess eagerly.

Mr. Barton shook his head reluctantly. He did not know where Sally was working now, but he felt sure she was still sharing diggings with Miss Frimp and Miss Fleming.

His loyalties lay with Sally, and Sally had not wanted the marquess to know her whereabouts.

"I don't even know where she's working," said Mr. Barton, glad to be able to tell part of the truth. "I warned her that jobs were hard to find in Fleet Street."

"But her home?" protested the marquess. "Her parents?"

"Don't know," said Mr. Barton. "I really don't know. She never spoke of them."

The marquess finished his beer. Another dead end. He began to wonder if he would ever see her again.

At that very moment Sally was, in fact, not very far away, working at her job and hating every minute of it.

She was the household editor of the *London*

Gentlewoman, a small glossy monthly magazine that did not have the distinction of being on Fleet Street or even beside it but was down one of those back alleys near Blackfriars Underground Station.

Sally had accepted the job because it was the only one she could get on short notice, the pay was reasonably good, and they did not know she had been previously employed as Aunt Mabel, Mr. Barton having given her a glowing reference as having been employed by him as household editor.

She discovered she was not a very domesticated girl, but she was a conscientious journalist and worked hard to supply her readers with hints on everything from the gentle art of potichomania—oriental-vase painting—to ornamental buttonwork.

She had just finished an article entitled *"How to Make a Summer Decoration for Your Fireplace."* She had raked up every idea she could, from simple fire paper—"Green is the best color for brightening up a room"—to shredded tartalan with a myrtle wreath. The magazine was read by an audience of ladies who would not dream of leaving their fireless fireplaces naked in

230

summer, and who felt compelled to dress them up with paper, material, looking glasses, or rustic fenders, and who loved to drape their mantels in snowy folds of point lace.

Sally was faced with working on her first knitting pattern for a cardigan. To Sally knitting was of the same vein as higher calculus—totally incomprehensible. A wool company had supplied her with some information, and she was laboring over the instructions, which meant nothing to her at all, but which she hoped her readers would be able to transform into a cardigan.

It was only after she had translated the first page of the wool company's instructions that Sally realized she had lost the second. She looked at the clock frantically. It was six-thirty on a Saturday evening. The company would be closed, and the article had to go to press that night. Now, the editor, Miss Huntley, was a stickler for method, discipline, and accuracy, and loved hinting that any suggestion of a lack of them would result in dismissal, and so Sally decided to do the best she could. Had the directions been "repeat this row forty times" or had they said fifty? Perhaps eighty? One hundred on the other hand sounded like a good round number, and it was only a sleeve anyway, and sleeves were surely not desperately important—and—Oh!, who cared anyway when one's heart was one large ache and the days dragged their weary length along.

She finished it quickly, through half-closed eyes, feeling that if she did not look very closely at what she was writing, it would somehow turn out all right. After all, the magazine had a small circulation, and she had never seen anyone actually reading it.

The marquess wandered into the library of Banjahar Palace, wondering what he was doing, moping uselessly about his parents' home.

Mr. Worthing, the secretary, was engaged in dealing with the day's correspondence with his usual admirable patience, since most of it was what he considered privately a waste of time. The duke had been in one of his complaining-about-everything moods since he had recovered from his latest infatuation, and had sent long and very boring letters to every dignitary in the county, complaining of everything from the state of the roads to the decline of the lesser-crested grebe. The people who had received his complaints had written back equally as long and boring explanations, to which the duke in turn had dictated long and boring replies, which, Mr. Worthing felt sure, would elicit even more boring and longer letters, and so it would go on until the duke fell in love with someone else.

Mr. Worthing was glad to see the marquess, who always had a pleasant word for him and who would sometimes sit down and pass a quiet hour or two discussing books. He was the only member of the household who seemed at all interested in the family library. Now Mr. Worthing was watching the marquess pacing up and down restlessly, and it dawned on him that his lordship had been troubled and upset for some time.

Mr. Worthing communed with himself briefly. He wondered whether to remark on his lordship's demeanor, and then decided it might be taken as stepping out of line. After some moments he contented himself by asking, "Can I be of assistance?"

"I wish you wouldn't say that," snapped the marquess. "It reminds me of Aunt Mabel. That was her stock phrase."

"I found Aunt Mabel a very pleasant old lady," ventured Mr. Worthing.

"I can't get her out of my head," said the marquess, suddenly sitting down and burying his head in his hands.

Mr. Worthing had felt that his post at Banjahar Palace had placed him beyond shock, what with the eccentricities of the marquess's parents and their various houseguests, but he had to admit to himself that the marquess had shocked him. Imagine such a handsome man as Lord Seudenham pining over an old lady! Well, George IV had had a penchant for older ladies, and there was . . .

The marquess looked up suddenly and caught the expression on the secretary's face and smiled ruefully. "No, Mr. Worthing. It's not what you think. Aunt Mabel was, in fact, a young girl called Sally Blane, hiding under a white wig and behind a clever set of rubber wrinkles and false eyebrows."

"My lord!"

"And not content with that, she masqueraded as Lady Cecily at the ball."

"Oh, dear!" said Mr. Worthing faintly,

remembering how cleverly Aunt Mabel had extracted the invitation from him.

"Exactly. And now I can't find her." Suddenly the marquess found it a relief to unburden himself and went on to tell the secretary about his search for Sally, his finding of the real Lady Cecily, and the dreadful day when he had embraced Miss Frimp.

Mr. Worthing hesitated and then said gently, "I would have thought, my lord, that a private detective could perhaps have found your young lady for you. She is probably working on some other publication in Fleet Street."

"But I don't know if I want to find her, dammit," said the marquess, getting to his feet and beginning to pace up and down again. "She lied to me. I've made such a fool of myself. What if she does not care for me? She can't, or she would have managed somehow to get in touch with me."

"Unless, of course," said the secretary, "the young lady was aware of your dislike of liars."

"Well, as a matter of fact, she is . . . because I told her. I even told her about that fake African explorer and said next time I came across a faker, I would turn him over to the police—or her."

"Then I should think that's the reason—"

"I don't *know* if that's the only reason. She may be engaged. She may not want me."

"I think," said Mr. Worthing cautiously, "that the young lady went to a great deal of effort and risk to engage your interest. Surely it would do no harm to find her and ask her. I know a very discreet inquiry agent—"

"Oh, forget it," said the marquess, his pride, as always, holding him back from another search. "I simply cannot bear to make a fool of myself again."

Mr. Worthing shook his head sadly, debated for a moment whether he should try to find the whereabouts of the mysterious Miss Blane himself, and decided against it.

"Why should she plague me so?" burst out the marquess. "Women are all the same. Celibacy is my trouble, pure and simple, and that can soon be remedied. I'm damned if I will waste any more time breaking my heart over some girl who doesn't care a rap for me."

Sally's monthly column appeared, and after three weeks had passed and no irate letters arrived from knitters, she breathed a sigh of relief. The knitting pattern must have been right after all.

Sally ploughed on with the household hints, learning for the first time what it was like to be tied to a job one detested.

And then the blow fell.

Miss Huntley, the editor, summoned her.

Sally opened the door of Miss Huntley's office timidly, feeling rather like a schoolgirl summoned to the headmistress's room.

Miss Huntley was holding with trembling fingers a crested letter, her face quite puce with anger.

"Miss Blane!" she commanded in terrifying accents. "Sit down!"

Sally complied, glad to sit down, as her knees were trembling.

"I have here," said Miss Huntley, "a letter from none other than Her Grace, the Duchess of Dartware."

"She doesn't know my name!" squeaked Sally, turning quite pale.

Sally's name did not appear at the top of the household column, which was by-lined "By a Lady of Quality."

"Don't interrupt," said Miss Huntley awfully.

"Of course Her Grace does not know your name. I will read her letter to you.

" 'Dear Editor, I followed your knitting pattern in the June issue and take leave to tell you that your so-called "Lady of Quality" is a moron. On completing the knitting pattern for the cardigan, I found the sleeves had been designed to accommodate an ape. They trail along the floor when I put the garment on. I hold you entirely responsible for a waste of time, money, and artistic effort. I shall tell all my friends that your publication is not to be trusted.' "

"Oh, dear," said Sally faintly.

"You have brought shame on my journal," said Miss Huntley wrathfully. "You will report to accounts and take your week's pay and *never darken my door again.*"

"But I shall write to Her Grace—"

"*Don't you dare!*" screamed Miss Huntley. "To be found out! To be accused of irresponsible journalism. And by a duchess!"

Sally got to her feet. She found she did not

much care. She hated the job anyway. Admittedly, she felt guilty because she should have told Miss Huntley that she did not understand the first thing about knitting, but it was very hard to tell the Miss Huntleys of the world things like that.

Without so much as a nod, she left the room.

All of a sudden Sally had a longing to go home to Emily. She felt she had failed to conquer London. She felt beaten and crushed by the perpetual weight of unrequited love. She longed for her mother. It was time to admit that she could not cope with life and to retire from London and hide in Emily's shadow.

Which shows how very miserable Sally was.

She had forgotten completely about the children.

CHAPTER EIGHT

August in London was broiling hot. The aristocracy fled to the coast, to France, to anywhere fashionable that guaranteed select company and cool breezes—with a few exceptions.

For example, the Marquess of Seudenham was still in town, seemingly unable to tear himself away despite the fretting protests of his new mistress, a certain voluptuous widow who had hoped for a free holiday in Deauville at least.

He was walking down Piccadilly one morning on the black blocks of shadow cast on the pavement by the shop awnings. He realized with a certain feeling of satisfaction that he had not thought of Sally Blane for one whole hour, and surely if he persevered, that hour could become a day and then a week, and the week could become . . .

"Paul!"

He looked down and found himself confronted by the small figure of his mother.

"Shopping," said his mother with a vague wave of her hand. "I'm buying wool—to knit you a jersey for Christmas."

"In August?"

"Why not? Believe me, it will take all that time to get it finished. And the charlatans who are producing knitting patterns cannot be trusted."

"Dear me," said the marquess vaguely. He did not often listen to anything his mother said.

"Yes. I was absolutely furious. I followed a knitting pattern for a cardigan in a magazine, and the woman who produced it must have been quite mad. The sleeves were a mile long when I finished."

"Dear me."

"Don't just stand there saying 'dear me' in that maddening way," snapped Her Grace. "I'm telling you about this knitting pattern."

"I'm listening now," said the marquess impatiently.

"I was saying that I followed this knitting pattern in the *London Gentlewoman,* and it was quite, quite nutty. I wrote to the editor and complained bitterly."

Knitting, thought the marquess with a reminiscent smile. Knitting and snow and the train.

"It's nothing to smile about," said his mother angrily. "Can you imagine any woman who has not the first idea about knitting calling herself a household editor?"

The marquess's gaze became suddenly intent. "What was the name of the magazine?"

"I'm glad to see you're taking an intelligent interest," said his mother acidly. "The *London Gentlewoman.*"

"I must go," said the marquess abruptly. " 'Bye, Mother."

"*Paul!* Aren't you even going to take me for tea?"

But the marquess was already striding off down Piccadilly. He bought a copy of the *London Gentlewoman* at a newsagent's stand and studied the address. He hailed a cab and directed the driver to Blackfriars, suddenly impatient, suddenly filled with hope.

It was a slender chance. . . .

You could have hired a detective if you really wanted to see her, nagged his mind. *You're better off without her.*

But nonetheless, despite the urgings of his intelligence, his emotions soon had him seated in Miss Huntley's office. That lady's face soon changed from a smile of gratified welcome to one of angry dismay when he explained he had come to discover the identity of the household editor of whom his mother had complained.

"You may tell Her Grace," said Miss Huntley, compressing her lips, "that as soon as I received her letter, I dismissed the household editor on the spot."

"That was very harsh of you," commented the marquess, taking a sudden acute dislike to Miss Huntley. She had a face like a sanctimonious sheep, and she needed a shave badly.

"Not at all! Not at all!" said Miss Huntley, quite agitated. "The integrity of this magazine must be upheld."

"Quite. Your household editor was not, by any chance, a certain Miss Sally Blane?" The marquess leaned forward, staring at Miss Huntley so intently that she shrank back a little in her chair.

243

"Well, as a matter of fact, she was."

"And where is she now?"

"I'm sure I don't know," said Miss Huntley repressively.

In the slow, measured tones of a man nearing the end of his tether, the marquess said, "Dear God! Everyone employs this girl without ever finding out her address!"

"Not in my case," said Miss Huntley huffily. "I demand that all employees furnish me with a full background."

"Then . . ."

"It is confidential information."

"Miss Huntley," grated the marquess. "I plan to marry Miss Blane, if she will have me. Now, run along and get me the information, or I will take your office apart . . . piece by little piece."

Miss Huntley opened her mouth, took one look at his face, and closed it again. Without a word, she scurried out of her office, returning shortly with a slip of paper.

"Now, my lord . . ." she began, but the Marquess of Seudenham was already off and running.

He drew a blank at the Bloomsbury address.

He would need to travel to Churchwold in Sussex.

But at Emily's prim villa a trim housemaid informed him that the family—including Miss Blane—had gone to Brighton for their annual holiday. She furnished him with the address of their rented house. The marquess drew a deep breath. Surely nothing could stop him from finding her now.

Sally was sitting among the pebbles on Brighton beach. The early evening light was turning the sea to pale gold. They had already had tea, but Emily was a great believer in keeping the children out in the fresh air as long as possible.

Baby Marmaduke had fallen asleep, his head lying on a pillow of sharp pebbles. Sally wondered whether to point out to Emily that it would be a good idea to give the baby a pillow, and then decided wearily that it didn't matter. Baby Marmaduke had fallen on his head so many times that his scalp must surely be as tough as leather.

The rest of the children were having splendid fun down at the water's edge, trying to drown each other. Sally hoped they would succeed.

Emily sat beside Sally, placid and content, her great cowlike eyes gazing out to sea.

Sally could never remember feeling quite so miserable in all her life. She berated herself for having given up her career so easily. She cursed the marquess for constantly invading her mind. The only bright spot on her horizon was the fact that her brother-in-law, George, had taken himself off somewhere and was not hanging around as he usually did, trying to find out the extent of her savings and asking her to hand them over.

Emily suddenly roused herself from her torpor and said, "You know, Sally, it's about time you thought of getting married. All this," said Emily with a sweep of her arm that encompassed beach and sea and children, "could be yours."

Sally looked thoughtfully to where Peter was kicking Paul, who had just hit Peter on the head with a rock. Mary and Joseph were sitting side by side in the water in their sodden clothes, crying dismally.

"I was discussing the matter with George, and he thinks it would be a good idea if you married his junior partner, Fred Binks."

"What!" screamed Sally. "Oh, *Emily*. He's got a receding chin and spots."

"Handsome is as handsome does," said Emily predictably. "He's a fine man. Be sensible, Sally. We can't really supply you with much of a dowry, and you're not exactly beautiful or anything." Beauty to Emily was a woman built along her own massive lines.

I was once, thought Sally dismally. *For one evening, I was beautiful.*

She closed her eyes briefly, remembering the snow and the feel of his lips against hers.

"Not that I don't notice a good-looking chap myself," Emily was droning on. "Now, take that fellow coming along the beach. Really splendid he looks. But you have to settle for what you can get, Sally."

Sally looked idly in the direction in which Emily had pointed. And then she slowly got to her feet while Emily stared up at her sister in amazement.

The Marquess of Seudenham came slowly along the beach, the sunlight gilding his black curls, his blue eyes vivid and intense in his tanned, handsome face.

Now, the marquess had planned all sorts of things to say to Sally when he found her—nasty things, wounding things, anything that might make her hurt as much as she had hurt him. But when he looked down at her thin, white, tired face and at the delicate lavender smudges under her eyes, he simply took her hands in his and said, "We're going to get married—as soon as possible."

He put an arm around her waist, and Sally rested her head on his shoulder.

She smiled up at him with her heart in her eyes. "Yes, Paul" was all she said.

He led her away along the beach, away from the screaming children, away from the startled eyes of Emily, his arm around Sally's waist and her head still lying on his shoulder.

" 'Scuse me, mum," said a red-faced man suddenly blocking Emily's view of the disappearing pair. "This 'ere your nipper?" He was holding a dripping wet and wailing Joseph in his arms. "Nearly drownded, 'e did. I rescued 'im."

"Then put him down," said Emily vaguely. "Oh, George!" she cried as her husband loomed over her. "Whatever shall we do? Sally's up and offed with a fancy man."

"What's his name?" demanded her husband. "Who is he?"

"I don't know," said Emily. "He's very, very

handsome. He said he was going to marry her, but they all say that before they ship them off to some terrible place like Turkey. Should I call the police?"

"That sister of yours is absolutely useless," snapped George. "Keeping her savings from me. She can go to Timbuktu for all I care!"

But Sally didn't.

She ended up being married with full ceremony at St. George's, Hanover Square, and society marveled over the bride's choice of bridesmaids as two elderly spinsters followed Sally down the aisle.

The Marquess of Seudenham entered his wife's bedroom on his wedding night and contemplated the vision that was Sally. She was sitting up in bed—reading.

"Darling!" he said. "How unromantic. What on earth are you reading? Birth control! Really, Sally, of all the books . . . Throw the damn thing away."

"But, Paul," wailed Sally, "think of the children we might have. Think of the jammy, sticky, kicking, screaming, demanding, children."

He gathered her in his arms and began to kiss

her so passionately that the book dropped from her suddenly nerveless fingers.

But fighting against her swimming senses, Sally freed her mouth from his and said, "But, *children!* Think, Paul!"

"Ours will be different," he said firmly, pulling her back into his arms and silencing her effectively with his kisses.

Ah, well . . . as Emily would have pointed out . . . we all think that.

Enter the world of regency England
with Marion Chesney, writing

Regency Romances

as *Jennie Tremaine*.

☐ **DAISY** Daisy Jenkins never expected to be admitted into the magic world of nobility until she meets her real father and discovers she's a lord's daughter! 11683-X $2.95

☐ **GINNY** Ginny Boggs, the daughter of a coal merchant, must prove that she is a real lady when she inherits a fortune from an aristocratic benefactor. 12820-X $2.95

☐ **LUCY** By winning a fortune at baccarat, lady's maid Lucy Balfour connives her way into London's most exclusive society and tries to win a handsome Viscount's heart! 15609-2 $2.95

☐ **MOLLY** Molly Maguire is a willful American with the brains, beauty and bravery to conquer London society. But will the stubborn Lord David Manley eventually conquer her?

15856-7 $2.95

☐ **POLLY** Pretty Polly Marsh always knew she could use her beauty as a passport into the circles of nobility where she felt she belonged. But would it get her the affections of the eligible Lord Peter? 17033-8 $2.95

Special Offer
Buy a Dell Book
For only 50¢.

Now you can have Dell's Readers Service Listing filled with hundreds of titles. Plus, take advantage of our unique and exciting bonus book offer which gives you the opportunity to purchase a Dell book for *only 50¢*. Here's how!

Just order any five books at the regular price. Then choose any other single book listed (up to $5.95 value) for just 50¢. Use the coupon below to send for Dell's Readers Service Listing of titles today!

DELL READERS SERVICE LISTING
P.O. Box 1045, South Holland, IL. 60473

Ms./Mrs./Mr. _____

Address _____

City/State_____ Zip _____

DFCA - 3/88